MIRANDA BARNES

# LOVE WILL FIND A WAY

*Complete and Unabridged*

## LINFORD
*Leicester*

First published in Great Britain in 2017

First Linford Edition
published 2018

A catalogue record for this book is available
from the British Library.

ISBN 978–1–4448–3778–0

Published by
F. A. Thorpe (Publishing)
Anstey, Leicestershire

Set by Words & Graphics Ltd.
Anstey, Leicestershire
Printed and bound in Great Britain by
T. J. International Ltd., Padstow, Cornwall

This book is printed on acid-free paper

# LOVE WILL FIND A WAY

Convalescing after a car accident, Gwen Yorke leases a remote cottage on the beautiful Isle of Skye. She hopes to find inspiration there for her career as a rug designer, and wants to decide if she and her boyfriend have a future together. In Glenbrittle, she finds herself drawn to the enigmatic, moody Andrew McIver, and his young daughter Fiona. To Gwen's delight, she and Fiona become close, frequently sketching together. But why is Andrew so unhappy about their friendship?

# 1

She studied his face, which was tired and angry-looking. There were times when she wondered about Rob, and their relationship. Like now, in fact.

'You don't have to do this,' he said wearily, pushing his coffee cup aside.

'I do.'

'What good will it do?'

She shrugged. 'Who knows? But I want to do it anyway. These past couple of months have been a nightmare, my life entirely disrupted. I want a break. I need to sort myself out.'

He thought for a moment and then said, 'You still blame me, don't you?'

'A little bit,' she admitted. 'That's why I want to have some time to myself.'

'I knew it! I knew you blamed me.'

Well, who else could she blame? She felt like asking that, but didn't. What good would it do?

Besides, it wasn't all Rob's fault. Not entirely. She was partly to blame herself. That was another reason she wanted to do this. She really did need to sort herself out.

'Where will you go?' he demanded.

'I'm not sure. But I'll let you know when I've decided.'

'Don't leave it too long,' he snapped, getting to his feet.

She wondered if it was a request or an ultimatum, but she didn't respond. She knew how upset he was. They had been together long enough for her to know that. Even so, she was determined to go ahead. She might well be accused of being wilful, but she was going to do it anyway. Something had to change. Her life was in ruins. That was what it felt like.

# 2

You didn't need to take a ferry to the island now. She knew that, but had forgotten, and she was disappointed when she saw the bridge in the distance. The final stretch by boat had always been the highlight of the journey to the Isle of Skye when she was a little girl. To reach the water's edge and then board the ferry to take them across Loch Alsh had been such a thrill. It didn't matter how many times you had done it. That feeling never went away. Sometimes — quite often, actually — the sea had been choppy, wild even, and the thrill that much greater.

Of course, the bridge had been in place a long time now, she thought with a wry smile, which only went to show how long it was since she had last been here. She drove on into the centre of Kyle of Lochalsh, where she pulled over. With eager anticipation, she got out of the car and made her way to the start of the road leading up to the bridge. She wanted to take a few photos to send home. Mum and Dad would be fascinated to see this modern way of crossing to the island.

Despite her initial disappointment upon seeing it, she had to admit the bridge was actually a rather beautiful construction. The elegant low arch swept effortlessly out across Loch Alsh, the gleaming white concrete shimmering in the late-afternoon sunshine. Regrettably, it was far too long for her to consider walking across to the other side. Certainly a mile or two, she thought. It was too late in the day, and after the long drive her wretched leg was playing up again.

Pausing for a moment, she gripped a handrail, closed her eyes, and screwed up her face to ward off the waves of pain. Then she steeled herself to limp a short distance up the approach road, from where she took a few photographs. On another day, she promised herself, she

4

would come back and take some more. Lots more, actually, she thought with grim determination.

As she snapped the camera back into its case, the weather suddenly changed dramatically. From out of nowhere, hailstones began to bounce off the footpath and rattle the metal railings alongside the road. She ducked her head in shock, and then glanced up to see a thin cloud that had crept across the sky but didn't look particularly threatening. She chuckled and hurried back towards the car.

That's Skye for you! she thought, as the hailstones pattered around her head. One surprise after another. But hadn't it always been like that?

Before she crossed the bridge, she turned into a little garage and filled up with diesel. The price per litre made her shudder, and she remarked on that as she paid her bill inside the little kiosk.

'Och, tell me about it!' the elderly man running the place said.

'It's ten pence a litre more than I'm

used to paying. Up here . . . well, it's just not fair. People are paying through the nose for one of the essentials of life in a remote rural area like this.'

'It's madness,' the man said, shaking his head. 'That's what it is.'

'I suppose it's the cost of the transport to get it here.'

'No way! That's no justification at all.'

'Then how is it justified?'

The man shook his head again. Then he took off his tweed flat cap and scratched his thinning thatch. 'It's just plain iniquitous,' he said finally, settling on his preferred word for it. 'We get the short end of the stick from everyone up here — London, Edinburgh, the oil industry. Everybody! And it always has been like that. It was no different when the great estates ran the country. And that's a fact!'

Deciding their conversation was in danger of slipping into a rant, Gwen looked for a way out. 'The bridge, though?' she suggested. 'You got the bridge, didn't you? That's progress, so far as ordinary folk are concerned.'

'The bridge? Aye. We got the bridge — eventually. But how long did we have to wait for it, eh? Hundreds of years. That's how long. Centuries!'

'Well, thank you for the diesel,' Gwen said, edging towards the door, wishing she'd not said anything in the first place.

'You're very welcome. Come back soon.'

Perhaps not, she thought as the door bell tinkled behind her. Not soon, anyway — not if she could help it!

And never again, she promised herself, would she dare to suggest to anyone that the price of things up here was too high. Lesson learned.

A beaten-up old Land Rover was standing at the far side of the forecourt. The driver was missing, but a little girl in the passenger seat caught Gwen's eye. With a pale face and long, dark hair, she was such a quiet, sad-looking little thing that you had to wonder about her. She seemed to be observing Gwen's progress intently, and when she saw Gwen looking at her, she gave a timid little smile and raised a hand to wave.

Gwen smiled and waved back. What a lovely child! she thought.

A black-haired young man, who looked to be in his thirties, walked up to the Land Rover and opened the driver's door. He got in and started the engine. The exhaust pipe rattled alarmingly and puffed out thick black smoke as the engine gave a throaty roar. The little girl gave Gwen a last wave before the vehicle sped off towards the bridge.

Gwen smiled happily, fatigue forgotten and her spirits quite restored. She got into her car, started the engine and, still smiling, set off in the tracks of the Land Rover.

# 3

The good feeling lasted as she drove across the island, heading for Glenbrittle. For a few miles the road stayed close to the sea as it skirted the lochs on the north side of the island. Then, at Sligachan, at the old climbers' inn, she turned off the main road to Portree and made her way inland, towards the south coast. Another couple of turnings, and another half-hour, and she was on the single-track road that led down into the glen. Then, suddenly, the Black Cuillins were there — right in front of her!

She stopped the car and gazed with delight at the long, jagged range of mountains running the length of the east side of Glenbrittle. Without doubt, she thought happily, they were the best mountains in the entire country. Always had been! They knocked Snowdonia and the Cairngorms, never mind the

Lakeland fells, into a cocked hat. No competition at all. There was nothing like the Cuillins anywhere else in the United Kingdom.

As she drove down the glen, her thoughts turned to the cottage and what lay ahead. Would Mrs McIver be there to welcome her? The good lady had said she would try to be, but given the uncertainty over her arrival time, Gwen thought it likely that she wouldn't. Not that it really mattered. Nothing would be spoiled. She was here for the whole of the summer, after all. Four-and-a-bit hopefully glorious months. There would be plenty of time for her to get to know Mrs McIver, and vice versa. A little uncertainty now, at the end of April, didn't matter in the slightest.

★   ★   ★

The cottage was at the far end of Glenbrittle, and very close to the beach. Gwen wasn't sure if she could really

10

remember it from long ago, as she liked to think, or if the pictures in her head all came from what she had seen of it more recently on various websites. Whichever was the case, she certainly recognised it when she saw it now.

The cottage was exactly how she had hoped it would be. *Tigh na Mara*, she recited softly to herself. *House by the Sea*. How lovely!

Stone-built, painted white, with a small copse of stunted pines close by, it fitted into the lower reaches of the hillside perfectly. It could have been there for centuries, and quite possibly had been.

As she headed up the rough approach track, Gwen shivered and smiled with anticipation. There was a little bit of apprehension, too, of course. When she got inside, would it still prove to be what she had been looking for, and hoping for? Oh, she did hope so!

A note addressed to her was inside a clear plastic envelope pinned on the front door:

*Dear Miss Yorke,*

*Welcome to Tigh na Mara!*

*I am so sorry to miss your arrival, but I'm afraid I have had to return to Portree for domestic reasons. I will come in the next day or two to see you. In the meantime, please visit the campsite and ask for Malcolm. He will give you the keys to the cottage, show you around and explain how everything works.*

*I do hope you enjoy your stay with us, and I look forward to meeting you very soon.*

*Yours sincerely,*

*Mary McIver (Mrs)*

Go to the campsite? Ask for Malcolm? Oh dear! What a nuisance, Gwen thought wearily, suddenly feeling deflated. If only she had managed to get here a bit earlier!

Still, she thought, turning around to look across the valley, the campsite was only a few hundred yards away and she could drive there. It was late, and she was too tired and achy to walk.

As she set off, she thought again that the campsite really was in a lovely location, so close to the beach, and with the peaks of the Cuillins towering behind. It was very quiet just now, too. She could see perhaps a dozen little tents spread across the site, and one or two camper vans. Still April, of course. Come the school holidays in the summer, it would no doubt be very different. It would be heaving then. Just as it always had been.

She nodded with satisfaction as she neared the entrance. It was exactly as she had remembered it. It was a real climbers' campsite, a place where people who wanted to climb the vast rock walls and ascend the great peaks came to marvel and to test themselves. It was just such a pity that she couldn't join them. Yet! she added firmly. Maybe one day . . .

The reception area for the site was in a timber building at the end of the rough track leading round past the toilet block. She parked and headed inside. A young man with long, untidy black hair sat behind the counter, working at a computer. She frowned, wondering why he somehow looked familiar. Then she shook her head. He couldn't be.

'Hello! My name's Gwen Yorke. I'm renting *Tigh na Mara* cottage, over the way there, for the summer. I've just arrived, and there was a note on the door telling me to come here and see someone called Malcolm about the key.'

The man looked over his shoulder at her and nodded. Then he stood up, picked an envelope from a shelf and dropped it on the counter in front of her.

'Key's in there,' he said. 'Watch out for the midges.'

With that, he turned and walked off into a back room. Gwen waited a few moments, but it didn't seem as if he was coming back anytime soon. She grimaced and made her way back to the car. Not very friendly, she thought with disappointment. Not quite the reception she had anticipated.

# 4

As she came out of the building, she saw the girl again. Of course! No wonder Malcolm had seemed vaguely familiar. He was the driver of the Land Rover in which the girl had been a passenger, back in Kyle of Lochalsh. So they'd come here too?

The girl was sitting on the steps at the entrance to one of two mobile homes that looked as if they might be the accommodation for staff at the campsite. Perhaps they lived here? It seemed likely.

The girl had seen Gwen, and seemed to recognise her. She stared intently and waved back when Gwen waved to her. Then she got up and came over to her.

'Hello again!' Gwen said with a smile. 'I've seen you before, haven't I?'

'Yes,' the girl said shyly. 'Just once, though.'

'That's right. At the garage.'

The girl nodded. 'My name is Fiona.'

'That's a pretty name. Mine is Gwen. Are you staying here, Fiona?'

'I live here. Does your leg hurt a lot?'

Gwen was taken aback, surprised. Shocked, almost.

'My leg?'

'You've got a bad leg, haven't you? Does it hurt a lot?'

'Not a lot, no. I did hurt it a while ago, but it's nearly better now, thank you.'

'Good.' Fiona thought for a moment and then added, 'Mine's better, too. Goodbye!'

'Goodbye!' Gwen replied with a smile as the little girl turned and walked away.

My goodness! she thought with amusement. What a funny, observant little thing you are, aren't you?

The front door to the cottage was a bit stiff, but she pushed harder and managed to get it open. Damp, she thought, sniffing, and then grimacing. Mrs McIver had said the cottage had

16

been empty over the winter. Here was the proof. A sticking door and that unpleasant musty smell. She would have to get some fresh air into the place.

Not when the midges were out, though. She hadn't forgotten how ferocious those little creatures could be when the conditions were right. Malcolm had been right to warn her. But it should be all right in April. July and August was their time. That was when they appeared in their countless billions on windless days to plague unhappy campers and walkers. Perhaps she would be acclimatised and resistant to them by then, though? Fat chance!

A quick tour of the cottage showed it was clean and tidy. It was also big enough and sufficiently well equipped for her needs. In fact, she thought with satisfaction, it was ideal. Just right. Perfect.

She decided to start bringing her stuff in from the car. That wouldn't take too long. After that, she would find something to eat, and . . . and just stop doing things! She had done quite enough for one day.

After unloading the car, she unpacked the groceries she had bought in Broadford, her first stop on the island, and made herself a ham sandwich. A bottle of water helped wash it down. Then she phoned home, wanting to get that over with before she collapsed with exhaustion.

'Yes!' she assured her mother. 'I really am here. And it really was a long drive — but I've made it.'

'All that way? It used to take us a few days to get there when you were little.'

'The roads are different now, Mum. Better. Much, much better. The cars are, too — though you'd better not say that to Dad!'

Her mother chuckled. 'You're right there. Well, take care, dear, and get a good night's sleep. You've earned it.'

'Yes, I think I have.'

'And be sensible, Gwen. Remember, you don't have to stay there if being on your own is too much for you. Somewhere like that can be very lonely, especially in bad weather.'

'Right, Mum. Be sensible. I shall remember that.'

'You can always come home, you know.'

'Yes, Mum! I do know that. But I want to do this, and I'm sure it will be fine.'

'I hope you're right. Don't let the midges get you down either!'

'There aren't any — not yet, anyway.'

'They'll come. Don't you worry.'

'Thank you, Mum. On that note . . . Say good-night to Dad for me.'

'If he wasn't down the allotment . . . '

'I know, I know. But it is important to him, isn't it? It's the seed sowing time. Anyway, good-night, Mum.'

She ended the call, smiling. To them, she knew, she was still their little girl. It wouldn't matter how old she became, it would always be like that, she supposed. Oh, she did love them, but it was nice to get away on her own for a while.

There was such a lot she wanted to do.

Besides, she had to get back to standing on her own two feet again. Her own two legs, rather, she thought with a grimace as she looked down at the one that was troubling her. That had to be her priority.

# 5

She was sorting out things in the bedroom when she heard a man's voice calling to her. It sounded as if he was at the front door. She called back and hurried downstairs.

'Oh, Malcolm! It's you. Hello again.'

He was standing in the doorway, holding on to the edge of the door. Surprisingly, he was smiling. In a very friendly way, and with a lilting Highland accent, he said, 'I just came to see how you were getting on, Gwen. Are you managing all right?'

She tried not to appear as astonished as she felt by the change of attitude.

'Yes, thank you, Malcolm. I seem to be doing fine. Well, I'm just unpacking, really.'

He nodded. 'Mother said to tell you she was sorry she wouldn't be here when you arrived. You'll have had a long day, I expect?'

'I have. Very long. And now it's catching up with me.'

'Leeds, isn't it? Where you're from?'

'Near there, yes. Just a little place, a village. You won't have heard of it.'

'You're probably right,' Malcolm admitted with a smile. 'Well, I won't take up any more of your time. I just wanted to see if you've figured out how things work in the cottage.'

Goodness! Was he offering help? What a change.

'I don't know yet how anything at all works — apart from the loo and the cold-water tap!'

He laughed. 'Well, I can soon get you started. May I come in?'

'Of course.'

She stood back and allowed him to enter.

He paused in the hallway and sniffed. 'The first thing to do, I would suggest, is to get some heat into the place. Nobody's been in here over the winter. So it's a bit chilly and damp, I'm afraid.'

'Oh? I hadn't noticed,' Gwen said, determined not to admit to finding fault with the cottage on day one.

'There's a wood-burning stove in the kitchen,' Malcolm said. 'I'll show you how to get that started. Then I'll show you where the immersion heater is, and one or two other things. But if we get the stove going, it will soon warm the place up. Keep it going, and it will lift that damp, mouldy smell. There's plenty of logs for you to burn.'

'Oh, that's good. Where are they?'

'In the shed out the back. Until you get things warmed up, I would suggest using the halogen heater as well. But you won't need that once the stove gets going.'

As Malcolm took her through the cottage, pointing out things she needed to know, Gwen began to relax. Her first impression of him had been a poor one, she conceded, but now he was being wonderfully friendly and helpful. She decided she must just have caught him at a bad moment when she arrived.

We all have them, she thought.

Perhaps things had gone wrong during the day for him. Or perhaps he had been trying to sort the computer out, and had been thoroughly immersed in what he was doing. Her arrival would have been an unwelcome distraction in that case. She knew how frustrating it could be when someone demanded attention when you were in the middle of something complicated that needed all your focus.

She watched now as Malcolm busied himself at the stove, setting kindling alight and placing logs he took from a basket in the hearth. It was useful to see how he did it. She didn't think she had ever started a fire herself. Malcolm obviously had. Soon the dancing flames took hold of the log and altered colour, going from yellow to blue to red in a cheerful, lively sequence.

'There,' he said at last, getting back to his feet, studying the blaze with satisfaction. 'She's away nicely.'

'That's lovely, Malcolm. I can feel the heat already.'

'It will soon warm the place up — this room, at least. The rest of the cottage will take a bit longer.

'Mum hasn't been so well lately, and she has Dad to look after, or she would have been in and lit the stove for you herself. And I was too busy to get over here earlier, unfortunately.'

'Oh, that's all right! Don't worry about it. I'm pretty hardy. I can rough it with the best of 'em. I did wonder, in fact, about camping for the summer, but I decided that would be too much.'

Malcolm smiled. 'Indeed it would. When the rain sets in here it's too much for anyone to be under canvas for more than a day or two.'

'Rain in summer?'

'Oh, yes. July can be pretty wet.'

She had forgotten about that, about how many days had been lost to rain during family visits in the school holidays.

'And then there's the midges?' she said with a rueful smile.

'Indeed. You've heard about them, have you?'

'I certainly have. You can't mention Skye to anyone who's ever been here without the midges coming up in the conversation. Anyway, I used to come here with my parents when I was little. So I remember them. And now you've reminded me, I remember the rain as well.'

'Yet you've still come back?'

She chuckled. 'Oh, I have plenty of good memories from those days. They are what brought me back.'

'Thank goodness for that,' Malcolm said, laughing. 'Right,' he added. 'The stove's going fine now, and I think I've told you about everything else. So I'll leave you to it, if you don't mind. There's jobs I need to do back at the campsite. If you do need anything, by the way, you know where to find me. Just ask at Reception if I'm not there.'

'You're there all the time, are you?'

'I am. For the summer, at least. But anyone there will help. It doesn't have to be me.'

'Well, I appreciate you coming to see

me, Malcolm. You've shown me how everything works, and you've got the stove going nicely. I can't thank you enough.'

'My pleasure.'

He smiled and headed for the door. She was tempted to ask him what had been wrong when she first arrived, but decided that wouldn't do. Whatever it had been, it was his business. Nothing to do with her. Besides, the awkwardness was gone now. Malcolm was a very nice man, after all, it seemed.

All she needed to do now was get her head down and sleep, if her throbbing leg would let her. It had been a long, tiring day, and she'd just about had enough of it. Too long, really. She would have been wise to break her journey instead of pressing on, desperate to see the Isle of Skye again. Well, I'm here now, she reminded herself happily. And I wouldn't be anywhere else.

# 6

She was up bright and early the next morning. Sun and a blue sky, together with a good night's sleep, worked their magic. She felt happy. After a quick breakfast, and armed with a mug of coffee, she began sorting out how she was to live and work for the next few months.

Where should she put things? And where was the best place to sit and think? And to create something new? All that, and more. She was determined this was going to be a productive summer, as well as time spent enjoying the Cuillins and building up some strength in her poor leg.

The cottage was a very simple little building. Most of the ground floor was taken up by a large living room, with a big farmhouse table and a galley kitchen part of it. A brick extension housing a modern bathroom had been added at some point, and beyond that there was a small, lean-to timber structure that served as a scullery-cum-mudroom. No doubt, she reflected, a place to leave wet coats and muddy boots was very necessary during the long, wet winters they would have here.

Upstairs there were two bedrooms, plus a surprisingly large walk-in cupboard attached to the larger bedroom that was a wonderful storage space. So there really wasn't a lot to consider. It was obvious how the space should be organised and used. She nodded with satisfaction.

At one time the cottage would no doubt have housed an enormous extended family, with elderly grandparents and perhaps other ancients, as well as umpteen children to be fitted in somehow. Now, though, there was just enough room for her and the things she was going to need over the next few months.

She would sleep in the smaller of the

two bedrooms, the one facing the sea. The larger bedroom, with the north-facing window, she would use as her work room, her studio. Her storage room, at least. If past practice was anything to go by, she would probably end up doing most of her work on the kitchen table. Being close to the kettle and coffee was an important consideration — a priority, in fact.

All that sorted, she decided to venture out for a little walk. She wanted to see how Glenbrittle looked this morning. She also wanted to stretch her aching leg and see if she could shake off some of the stiffness from her long drive the previous day. Building up the muscles in her leg was going to be a long, continuous process that started right here and now.

\*　\*　\*

Disappointingly, she couldn't see much of the mountains. The entire Cuillin range was wrapped in thick, dark cloud above about five hundred feet. No surprise there, she thought with a wry smile. She knew from experience that high mountains seemed to generate their own cloud and rain, the Cuillins as much as any of them. But with luck, and if the sun did its job, the murk might clear in a couple of hours.

Already the sun was lighting up the little beach and the bay beyond. She smiled with joy as she reached the edge of the low dunes and gazed out across the bay. The tide was receding fast, leaving behind an expanse of wet sand that gleamed and glistened enticingly in the morning sunlight. Beyond the beach, the alluring islands of Rum and Canna looked almost close enough to touch. And was that Eigg there, as well? And Muck?

No. Perhaps not. It wouldn't be possible to see all the Small Isles. Be happy with the two you can be sure of, she admonished herself with a chuckle.

So wonderful, she thought happily. Oh, this is why I came here! It was exactly as she remembered it from all those years ago.

The mountains might be beyond her now, she had to admit, but one day she hoped to be able to venture up them again. Even if she couldn't do that, she would enjoy what she could do, and what she could see. Of that, she was quite certain.

She walked out across the sand to the water's edge. Then she turned and strolled along beside it, watching the little waves rippling towards her, each one reaching a little less far than the last. The tide was gently on its way out.

When she looked behind her, she could see the cottage plainly, its white-painted stonework standing out defiantly from the dark green backcloth of old grass and heather on the lower slopes of the hillside.

My cottage! she thought happily. Home? Why, yes. For now, at least.

When she reached a large patch of low-lying rock festooned with slippery green seaweed, she stopped and turned to walk back across the beach. By then, unfortunately, her leg was aching badly. The pain had started a little earlier but she had been able to ignore it for a time. Now, though, that was no longer possible. It was pulsing so strongly that it threatened to bring tears to her eyes. She would have to take the weight off and rest her leg.

If the sun had been stronger she might have been tempted to sit on the dry sand for a while, but the morning was too cool for that. Instead, she gritted her teeth and headed back towards the cottage, frustrated but promising herself it wouldn't always be like this. Her leg would heal. Already, she reminded herself grimly, it was so much better than it had been just a few weeks ago. Patience, she told herself sternly, not for the first time. That's what I need. More patience.

Back at the cottage, she looked for the painkiller tablets she used sparingly, and was gradually weaning herself off altogether. To go with two of them, she would have a mug of sweet tea, she decided. Something to make her feel better.

But that was easier said, or thought, than done. No water came out of the tap when she held the kettle under it. None at all.

Puzzled, disbelieving, she stared at the tap a moment, and then screwed it round as far as it would go. Still nothing. Just a few drips. Frustrated, she almost hurled the kettle across the room. What on earth . . . ?

She slumped down onto a chair. What was wrong? What had happened? She had no idea, she admitted, shaking her head. Advice, perhaps even a plumber, was needed.

Mrs McIver lived many miles away in Portree. It was no good asking her. Besides, the poor woman wasn't well, it seemed. The best thing would probably be to go to the campsite and speak to Malcolm again. See if he could help once more.

# 7

Fortunately, Malcolm was working in the campsite shop, stocking shelves with tins and packets of groceries from big cardboard boxes. Gwen was very relieved to see him there again.

'Good morning!' she called as cheerfully as she could manage.

He glanced over his shoulder at her. 'Hello. How are you?'

'Fine, just fine, thank you. I had a good night's sleep, and this morning I had a lovely little walk on the beach.'

'That's good,' he said, pulling out jars of jam from one of the boxes.

She waited a moment, watching him work, reluctant to interrupt, before saying, 'I've got another problem, I'm afraid. There's no water. The taps were working first thing this morning, but they're not now. Has there been a problem somewhere, do you know? A burst pipe, perhaps?'

He shook his head, but she didn't know if that meant 'no' or that he had no idea.

'I was wondering what you would advise me to do. Do you know a plumber? Or perhaps I should call your mother? What do you think?'

'I'll be over in a few minutes,' he said, his back still turned towards her, his work continuing without pause.

Gwen grimaced. 'Perhaps I should just call your mother? That would be more convenient, wouldn't it?'

'I'll come over.'

That seemed to be that. Seemingly, there was nothing more to be said.

Gwen turned to leave, wondering if she had somehow offended him. This offhand treatment was in such marked contrast to Malcolm's manner last night. It was just like it had been when she first arrived. The stress of the job? Perhaps he was just sick of the sight of her!

All the way back to the cottage she

wondered about it. Malcolm's unfriendly attitude had quite taken the gloss off the morning.

That wasn't entirely a bad thing, she thought with a rueful smile as she neared the cottage. At least it had taken her mind off the pain in her leg for a few minutes.

Oh well, she thought. Other people have problems, too. She wouldn't be the only one struggling this morning. Perhaps Malcolm just had too much to do, and too many problems to sort out. When it was like that, you had to focus on one thing at a time, get it done and tick it off the list. There was no other way.

That was probably why putting tins of baked beans and jars of jam on the shelf took precedence over her water tap, she thought with a reluctant grin. Perfectly understandable, really.

Back at the cottage, she felt the need to be purposeful, and to make a positive start on something. Some distraction therapy, she thought. That's what I need. Just forget my leg and the water supply — and the inconsistent Malcolm.

In the larger bedroom she moved the bed aside and dragged a small table in front of the window. Then she began unpacking her equipment and arranging it on the table. The laptop was one important item, but it didn't occupy pride of place in the centre. That was reserved for a large sketching pad and a box containing a hundred coloured pencils: artists' pencils.

The plan was to get back to basics, and to return to doing what she had started off doing: sketching and drawing. She had felt for some time that she had become too reliant on computers, and that her creativity had suffered as a consequence. During her time here, she wanted to get back to doing the simple things, and to allow the colours and textures of the Skye landscape to give her what she needed. She wouldn't have come otherwise.

'Hello!'

The call made her jump. She spun round. Malcolm — already?

'Coming!' she called.

He was poised uneasily on the threshold when she made her way awkwardly downstairs. She was embarrassed to see him watching her progress intently.

'I'm a bit stiff today,' she said apologetically.

He nodded. 'Mind if I have a quick look at the kitchen tap?'

'Of course not. Go right ahead.'

She avoided following him into the kitchen area. It seemed best to let him do what he wanted to do without having her looking over his shoulder. Besides, she wasn't sure how best to deal with him today. Not that she really cared about that, she told herself sharply. She just wanted her water back on. If Malcolm could arrange that, she would be eternally grateful.

He wasn't in the kitchen long. Just a minute or two, as if testing her complaint that there was indeed no water coming out of the tap. Then he brushed past her and went back outside. Moments later she caught a glimpse of him setting off up the hillside behind the cottage.

She shrugged, sighed, and turned to start putting a few things she had brought with her into the kitchen cupboards. There wasn't much to do. Soon, she decided, she was going to have to do a major grocery shop, which would probably mean a trip into Portree. If the water didn't come back on, that might well be today.

She could look up Mrs McIver while she was there, or search for a plumber herself. It didn't look as if Malcolm would be able to solve the problem, and she had no idea where he'd gone now. She wasn't going to look for him either. He wasn't very pleasant to deal with this morning. She sighed. She just didn't know where she stood with him.

Having had second thoughts about where she wanted to work, she started bringing her sketching materials downstairs and laying them out on the big table in the kitchen. Already she knew that was where she would want to be most of the time.

While she was upstairs, collecting more of her things, she heard Malcolm come back into the cottage. Moments later she heard a rush of water from the kitchen tap, and possibly from the bathroom too. Then she heard the toilet flush. She arched her eyebrows with surprise, and then nodded with relief. Things were looking up. The water seemed to be running again, thank goodness. Clever Malcolm!

'Thank you, Malcolm!' she called as she descended the stairs. 'We have water again. That's wonderful. But what was the problem?'

He seemed to be running his eye over her pencils and papers spread out on the table. Now he looked round at her and shrugged. 'The connection's a bit iffy, that's all. I'll get some new joints for it.'

'Oh? You mean . . . oh, I see! The water isn't from the mains. It comes from a spring or something, up on the hill? I never thought of that.'

He nodded and looked back at the table. 'You're going to do some drawing?'

'That's the idea,' she said with a smile.

He nodded again. It was as if he seemed to approve, she thought with surprise. It wasn't a matter of expressing polite interest. He was actually approving of her plan. What a cheek!

'It's what I do,' she added. 'For my work, I mean. My livelihood.'

'Good,' he said. 'You'll have to go easy on that leg,' he added after a moment.

She nodded agreement. But she was surprised again, and disappointed. She didn't want people here to think of her as disabled, or anything like that. If only he hadn't seen her coming down the stairs!

'I broke it,' she said. 'A while ago.

But it's pretty good now.'

'Yes,' he said, as if he could see that too.

He seemed to want to say something else, but he struggled for a moment to get it out. Then he gave up and turned to leave.

'My name's not Malcolm,' he said over his shoulder as he left.

# 8

That afternoon Mrs McIver arrived. It was the first time Gwen had had the chance to meet her face to face, although they had spoken by phone several times.

'I'm so sorry I could'nae be here to greet you when you arrived,' the good lady said. 'Unfortunately, I have a sick husband, and he's been very unwell these past few days. I had to get him away to the hospital again. And I wasn't so well myself, either.'

'Please don't apologise, Mrs McIver. Malcolm told me how things were. There was no problem at all. I got here, which was the main thing, and since then I've been sorting myself out, and finding out where everything is and how things work.'

'Malcolm helped you?'

'Er, yes,' Gwen said hesitantly, not

sure whether she should express her uncertainties about Malcolm. 'He did. Several times, in fact. He'll be sick of the sight of me, I'm sure! I've been badgering him with one problem after another, when he's so busy anyway.'

'Och, no! He'll no mind at all.'

Already Gwen was warming to Mrs McIver, just as she had thought she would. She seemed a lovely Highland woman, and from the sound of things she had plenty to keep her busy. Looking after a sick husband would be top of her priority list, but managing a holiday property would be demanding too. She wasn't a young woman.

'Now, have you discovered how everything works?'

'Yes, I think so, thank you. The cottage was a bit chilly when I arrived, but Malcolm came over in the evening and showed me how to light the stove. It was nice having it on, and it soon warmed things up. Today, it's lovely.'

Mrs McIver nodded. 'I warned you in advance the cottage needed warming up after the winter. You're a little bit early for us, and, unfortunately I couldn't get here myself to see to the stove.'

'Everything's fine, Mrs McIver! Please don't worry about that at all. The cottage is exactly what I wanted, and so far as the weather is concerned, I knew what I was letting myself in for before I came.'

Mrs McIver looked relieved. 'Well, if you say so, dear. Now, is the cottage sufficiently equipped for you? Is there anything missing?'

'Oh, no! Nothing at all. The cottage is perfect, thank you.'

'Well, I'll be getting along, then. But, remember, if there is anything you need, don't hesitate to ask Malcolm. If he can't sort it out himself, he'll call me, and between us we'll get it done.'

After further similar exchanges, Mrs McIver began to edge towards the door. She had a sick husband to see to back in Portree, and Gwen sensed she was anxious to be on her way. She wouldn't hold her up any more.

'I hope your husband is feeling better soon, Mrs McIver.'

'So do I, dear. So do I. When I get back to Portree, I'll visit him in the hospital to hear what they have to say this time.'

No mention of what exactly it was that was ailing Mr McIver. Gwen hoped it was something trivial, although that seemed unlikely. Mr McIver's illness seemed to be a long-running or recurring condition.

'Now, is there anything else before I go?'

Gwen thought for a moment and shook her head. 'No, nothing at all, thank you. You've been very kind.'

But then she did think of something.

'Actually, there was something I would like to raise with you.'

'Yes?'

Gwen hesitated, wanting to make sure that what she wanted to say came out right.

'Well,' she said, taking a deep breath, 'as Malcolm was leaving this morning, after fixing a problem with the water supply, he said something that puzzled me. He said his name wasn't Malcolm.'

Gazing at Mrs McIver, she added, 'I haven't got it wrong, have I? I mean, you call him Malcolm. But does he prefer people outside the family to use another name?'

'Och! I'm so sorry about that.' Mrs McIver chuckled. 'I should have warned you. I just didn't think. It must have been Andrew you met this morning, Malcolm's twin brother.'

Gwen's hand flew to her mouth with surprise. 'Oh! Really?' After a moment she began to laugh. 'How extraordinary! Why didn't I think of that?'

'Andrew isn't usually here very much, you see. It's Malcolm that runs the campsite. Andrew is just helping out at the moment.'

'I see. Well, that explains something that was bothering me a lot. Thank you, Mrs McIver.

'Do you know, I never guessed I was dealing with two different people. I just thought Malcolm sometimes behaved and spoke differently, as if he was a rather moody person. I even wondered if he had a divided personality.'

'A lot of folk wonder that,' Mrs McIver said, with a twinkle in her eye. 'They think I've got one fine son, when I've actually got two. They may look exactly alike, but they're quite different people. Still, it sounds as if you've seen enough of them to realise that for yourself.'

Gwen laughed. 'Mrs McIver, you've set my mind at rest! I thought it was something about me that was giving Malcolm difficulty.'

'Oh, no! Don't you ever think that. You're fine, dear.'

*   *   *

How stupid of me! Gwen thought afterwards, chuckling and shaking her head. Why didn't I think of that? It's incredible that they appear so much alike, though. They really are identical.

I must look more closely when I next see them — one of them, at least. There must be some way of distinguishing between them.

She laughed again, gave a final shake of her head, and moved on. There were things she wanted to do before the afternoon was over.

# 9

The next day Gwen decided her main aim would be to manage a little walk to the far side of the bay, and perhaps a short distance along towards the headland. Not far, though. Yesterday had been a warning. She wasn't going to overdo it. For now, at least, she would be happy if she could walk a hundred yards further today than she could yesterday. Then, tomorrow, her target would be another hundred yards. Not forgetting, she reminded herself, that an extra hundred yards would actually be an extra *two* hundred yards, given that she would have to walk all the way back again.

She smiled, thinking she was starting to sound like an accountant or a book-keeper, though counting yards instead of pennies. But that was what she was, and how she wanted it to be.

Making progress, and measuring it, was what she wanted to do every single day. It was the only way back to where she wanted to be. She knew she wouldn't wake up one morning and suddenly find her leg was perfectly all right again, without her having done anything very much to bring that about. She was going to have to work at it, if she was ever to be able to do again the things she used to do.

It was no good wishing the accident hadn't happened, either. She just had to cope with its legacy, and she was determined to do just that. No gain without pain, she reminded herself. It seemed a familiar phrase. Somebody famous must have said that once, and she was sure they were right, whoever they were.

Just as she was setting out, the sun appeared and lit up the sea, the beach, and even the chain of mountains behind the campsite. She smiled with satisfaction. How wonderful! A perfect start to the day.

The tide was high, so she didn't bother going down onto the beach. Instead, she made her way along the sandy track that gave access to the campsite. She went as far as the point where the track turned inland, towards the reception centre, and then she struck up behind the toilet block, heading for the path that ran the half-dozen miles from there to Rubh' an Dùnain, as the map suggested the headland was called.

The going was difficult for her. She followed a path, a path of sorts, but it was a very rocky one with few flat, level stretches. So it was a matter of feeling her way along, threading a course between and over the boulders and jagged rocks. After a few minutes she paused for breath and looked around. On the far side of the bay she could see her cottage. It was in shadow from the hill behind it at this time of day, but it still looked very pretty and homely.

My cottage! she thought with a wry smile. Not really. But for now, it was.

She watched the sea trying to reach a little higher on the beach, without quite managing it. Each little wave petered out at the very edge of the wet sand. Not an inch further could it reach. The tide was on the turn, she realised, and about to start the long retreat that would expose the length of the beach once again.

Over on the campsite there were a few people moving about between the dozen or so tents. In a few weeks there would be many more of both, but now, at the start of the season, only a few hardy campers were here. Serious walkers and climbers, probably, and perhaps a few birdwatchers too.

Then she spotted Malcolm — or Andrew! Which of them was it? She watched intently as the distant figure went about its business, but she couldn't decide. They even dressed the same, she noted. She hadn't noticed that before, but they did. Black jeans and a heavy navy sweater seemed to be their preferred wear. Their black, untidy hair was the same, too. Was it the result of deliberate agreement or just unself-conscious behaviour that somehow produced a consensus? Perhaps there was still some sort of bond between them, forged in the womb, of which they were unaware?

They seemed fascinating questions. Appearance was one thing, but what about other possible connections between them? Conceivably, lifelong connections. Would they each know, or sense, what the other was feeling, for example? She had never known identical twins before, and she had no idea.

I must study them, she thought with a wry smile. It will give me something else to do. Make field notes and come up with a theory: *Results of the Andrew and Malcolm McIver Investigation.*

Malcolm or Andrew — whichever one it was — took some rubbish to one of the big commercial bins lined up neatly against a fence. He lifted the lid and dropped a couple of black bags inside. Then he bent to pick up a stray bit of paper, which followed the bags into the bin. Andrew, she thought. The man who had fixed her water supply. The practical one. That's exactly what he would do.

But when the figure below walked across twenty feet of grass to speak to a couple emerging from a small tent, she changed her mind. Malcolm! she decided with a grin. The chatty one, the sociable one. That's who it is.

She shook her head and, still smiling, moved on. Malcolm or Andrew? What a puzzle! They were a perfect enigma. Perhaps in time she would be able to tell which of them she was looking at, but not yet she couldn't.

She would have to ask Mrs McIver how she did it — always assuming she *could* do it . . . oh, tosh! Of course she could. A mother, any mother, would always know which of her children she was looking at. And Mrs McIver would certainly know. But it would be interesting to know how she did it, all the same.

For now, though, she wouldn't ask her. She would just see if she could work it out for herself.

A little further along the path, she stopped again to rest. It really was proving very difficult to make progress. The path was hard going anyway, as it made its way over rocky ground, but now it was dipping in and out of little ravines as well. She just didn't have the strength in her bad leg to negotiate them easily. At times she was reduced to using her hands and knees.

She began to think she had been overly optimistic. Perhaps she should have concentrated at first on walking on the flat. The beach and the fields in the bottom of the glen might have been a better place to start rebuilding her fitness.

For a few minutes she sat on a big, flat rock and let herself recover, glorying in the view across the bay and the shimmering surface of the sea. A flock of white birds, gulls of some sort, were concentrating their efforts on a patch of water a couple of hundred yards offshore. She watched as they dived repeatedly into the sea and came back up again, sometimes to rest on the surface. At times the closely-packed flock of birds resembled a ball that was moving slowly across the surface of the sea. She guessed they had found a shoal of small fish they were following and feeding from.

The birds suddenly disappeared from view, overtaken by a wall of grey cloud that was moving fast across the bay, and heading towards her. It had come from nowhere. One moment she could see the far side of the bay, and her cottage, and the next there was only this fast-moving grey curtain that looked as if it was bringing rain.

She struggled to her feet, alarmed by the speed of the approaching cloud. It was time to turn back anyway. She had walked far enough. More than enough, in fact. Her bad leg was throbbing, and even her good leg was feeling tired and weak. Now it looked as if she was in for a soaking, as well.

As soon as she set off, she realised she should have turned back sooner. She was even more tired than she had realised. It was hard to lift her feet over rocks on the path, and her knees felt ready to give way on her. Goodness! What had she done?

Then the cloud enveloped her, bringing with it a fierce squall of driving rain to batter and confuse her. Within moments she was very wet indeed. She could feel rainwater trickling down her neck, down inside her jacket and shirt to her back. Her trouser legs were sodden. Inside the lightweight fabric boots she wore, her feet were squelching.

Not good, she thought grimly as she stumbled on. Not good at all. I should have had more sense than to let myself get into this predicament. It's ridiculous. I'm not even in the mountains!

Things got worse when she slipped as she made her way down into one of the little ravines she had crossed on her outward journey. Then it had been difficult. Now it was much worse. She fell and landed heavily on her shoulder. At least it wasn't my head, she thought as she grimaced and lay still for a moment to recover.

When she had got her breath back, she began to rearrange her collapsed body. Ignoring the pain from her legs and shoulder, she turned onto her hands and knees, and began to clamber out of the ravine.

As she reached the top of the slope and began to wonder how she might manage to get off her knees and back onto her feet, she heard a voice nearby say, 'Well, that's one way to do it!'

# 10

Gwen turned her head and peered at the figure looming over her. It was a young woman, she could see that much. The woman was dressed in proper walking gear, had a rucksack on her back, and looked quite comfortable in the wind and rain.

'Are you all right?'

Gwen nodded and managed to eke out a reply while fighting back tears brought on by the pain in her leg and the feeling of utter haplessness brought about by her collapse.

'Yes, thank you,' she stuttered. 'I'm all right. Well, not entirely, no. Not at this moment, I mean. I fell — and it bloody well hurts!'

'Anything broken, do you think?'

Gwen shook her head, took a deep breath and rallied. 'Not this time,' she said with a wry smile. 'I'm just a bit more battered and bruised.'

'Here, let me give you a hand.'

The woman leant down, took Gwen's hand and wrapped an arm around her back. 'Up you come!'

With her help, Gwen struggled back to her feet. 'Thank you,' she gasped. 'I slipped, I think. Went down with a bit of a crash.'

'It's easy done.' The woman peered at her anxiously. 'Just take a moment. Sit down on this rock and get your breath back. In fact . . . ' She slipped the rucksack off her back, rummaged in a side pocket and brought out a flask. 'In fact, have a cup of coffee. It's not up to much, I'm afraid, but it is warm still.'

'Oh, no thank you!' Gwen said. 'I couldn't possibly take your coffee.'

The woman ignored her and filled the cup she took from the top of the flask. 'We'll share it,' she announced, handing Gwen the cup. 'I have some painkillers somewhere in my rucksack, as well.'

'No, thank you,' Gwen said firmly. 'I have my own, actually, but I'm trying to wean myself off them.'

'Your leg, is it?' the woman asked, glancing down at Gwen's lower half. She had obviously figured out the root cause of the problem.

'It is, yes. I broke it. At least, a car did. A bad accident. But I'm on the mend now.'

'I can see that. You wouldn't have got this far a month or two ago, I bet.'

'No. You're right. I've made a lot of progress.'

'Good for you. I'm Ellen Cavendish, by the way.'

'Hello, Ellen. Gwen Yorke.'

They nodded and smiled at one another. Gwen took a sip of coffee and handed the cup back. 'Thank you. That was lovely.'

Ellen chuckled. 'Hardly. It was made first thing this morning, but it's still quite warm. On a day like this, anything warm is welcome, isn't it?'

Gwen shivered. 'You're right. And I'd better get moving. Where have you come from?'

'Loch Coruisk.'

'Oh? That's on the other side of the mountains, isn't it?'

'It is, yes. I camped over there for a couple of nights.'

'Really?' Gwen was impressed. 'So which way are you going now?'

'Back towards the campsite. You, too?'

'I am, yes. This is quite far enough for me for one day. Too far, in fact.'

'Easy does it. You need to build up some strength in that leg of yours.'

'You're right. That's a large part of why I'm here, actually.'

As they set off walking, Gwen realised that the rain had ceased and the wind had dropped. The cloud was fast clearing away, too. It had just been another squall, a short-lived little storm. She was thankful it hadn't been the onset of the kind of weather front that would have let them in for two or three days of heavy rain.

'What was the weather like where you were camping?' she asked.

'Pretty good most of the time. I didn't see any rain at all until this morning. It was just cold and bright.'

'Were you alone?'

'Oh, yes. I needed to get away from people for a while.'

'It sounds like you chose the right place to go.'

Ellen laughed. They moved on together, but slowly. That worried Gwen. 'I don't want to hold you up,' she said.

'Don't worry about that. I'm just about all walked-out myself.'

Gwen suspected her companion was just being polite, but there was nothing she could do about it. She certainly couldn't walk any faster. At least the pain from her leg didn't seem so bad now, though. Moving was helping. But she suspected she would have a rough night as her leg stiffened. Still, she could always take one of the pills she had brought with her if she had difficulty sleeping.

'Where are you staying?' Ellen asked.

'Here in Glenbrittle. At the campsite.'

'Oh? Lovely. You've not got far to go, then.'

'Thankfully. Are you one of the hardy folk with a tent at the campsite?'

'Oh, no! Not me. I'm done with camping for the moment. It was just a couple of days off I had. I live in Portree,' she added, 'and have done all my life. I work there, too — in a bank.'

'I envy you.'

'Which part?' Ellen asked with a chuckle. 'Working in a bank?'

'Oh, no. I couldn't do that. I would be most unsuitable. By the second day I would be insulting all the customers.'

'It's hard not to at times, I must admit. Our wonderful customers are not all reasonable people.'

'I envy you living on Skye, though. That was what I meant.'

'Well, increasingly often I've thought of leaving, and venturing out into the big, wide world. But it hasn't happened yet. Where are you from yourself?'

'Near Leeds. A village not far from the city.'

'So you're on holiday? Or should I make an inspired guess and say convalescent leave?'

Gwen laughed. 'A bit of both, actually. But I want to do some work as well.'

'Where are you staying?'

'I've rented a cottage for the season.'

'Oh? That sounds interesting. So what kind of work do you do?'

'I'm a rug designer. My time here will let me know if I'm capable of working away from home. Who knows? I might like it here so much I don't want to leave.'

The women got on well together and their conversation took Gwen's mind off her problems. She even forgot how tired she had been when Ellen arrived on the scene. In no time at all, it seemed, they were back at the campsite. Just beyond, facing the sea, Ellen had parked her car. They paused nearby.

'Well, it was lovely meeting you,'

Gwen said. 'And thank you so much for your help.'

Ellen smiled. 'The only help you needed was a sip of lukewarm, muddy coffee.'

Gwen laughed. 'Are you just going back to Portree now?'

'I am, yes.'

'Well, would you like to come back to the cottage first, and have a mug of hot chocolate or coffee with me?'

'Yes, I would. Thank you, Gwen. That would be lovely. I just need to see them in the campsite office first. Then we can drive over. I won't be a minute, if you want to wait for me?'

'Of course.'

Ellen used the remote to open the car doors. 'I just need to see Malcolm about something for tonight. I'll be right back.'

Malcolm? Gwen thought. That's interesting.

# 11

The cottage smelled and felt a lot better now the stove had been going. The gentle warmth had gradually dispelled that cold, damp, mouldy air that had greeted Gwen when she first arrived.

'Come on in,' she said, holding the door open wide for Ellen. 'Let's get our wet things off and warm up a bit.'

'Ah, warmth! It's lovely in here,' Ellen remarked as she stepped inside and stooped to take off her boots.

'It is now. It wasn't when I first arrived, though. But Malcolm, from the campsite, came over to light the stove for me. I've kept it going ever since.'

'So you've met Malcolm?'

'Oh, yes. He's a lovely guy, isn't he?'

'I think so,' Ellen said with a smile. 'This is his mother's cottage, by the way, isn't it?'

'Yes. I'm renting it from her.'

'I've never been inside before, but it seems very comfortable — now the stove's going so well, at least.'

'It is. Perfect for me. Just what I wanted. Have a look round while I make our hot chocolate — or would you prefer coffee?'

'Coffee, I think. Thanks.'

'I think I'll have coffee, as well, then.'

Ellen began to wander around as Gwen set to work filling the kettle and bringing out the things she needed. 'Instant all right for you?'

'Perfect. It really is a lovely little cottage, isn't it? How long did you say you have it for?'

'Only for the summer.'

'Only . . . ?' Ellen broke off and laughed. 'Don't you start teasing me already!'

'It's true,' Gwen said apologetically. 'I'm here for the summer. Lucky me, eh?'

'Lucky you indeed!'

Gwen made the coffee and took the mugs across to the big table. 'Here or a

70

comfortable chair?'

'Here's fine.'

'Good. Those armchairs by the stove are the sort that I find difficult getting out of with my leg problem. At the moment, at least.'

'And I'm so tired,' Ellen confessed, 'I'd probably fall asleep if I sat in one of them.'

Gwen didn't believe a word of it. Ellen seemed to be a very fit woman. She could probably walk another twenty miles without feeling overly tired.

'You know, Gwen,' Ellen said, sipping her coffee, 'you really are doing very well. I admire you. Using your leg, doing little walks, is exactly what you should be doing. Resting it would do no good at all. Keep it up and you'll soon be up and running again.'

Gwen smiled. 'Thank you. I don't suppose I would ever be able to keep up with you, though. You're obviously very fit.'

'Oh, it's the life we lead here. You'll

be very fit, too, by the end of the summer.'

'I hope so.'

'You said it was an accident? Your leg, I mean?'

'Yes. Car crash. But it wasn't me driving.'

She didn't expand on her answer. She didn't want to talk about it. There was no need. The car crash was over and done with. She was on the mend. No need for explanations to someone she didn't know.

'Have you always lived here, Ellen?'

'Here, or hereabouts. So I've been climbing and walking all my life.' She chuckled and added, 'Living on Skye, you have to embrace the outdoor life. There isn't much else you can do.'

'It shows, too. I envy your fitness. I mean, I'm not a gym freak, or anything, but I would love to be in the shape you're in.'

'With my wrinkles and weather-beaten face, you mean?'

Gwen chuckled and shook her head.

'No, not at all! I just meant how strong and athletic you are.'

'Oh, you should have seen me when I was eight years old. That was when I was in peak condition — before I got fat and heavy.'

Gwen laughed. Fat and heavy? She didn't think she had ever met anyone who was less like that. She sipped her coffee, feeling pleased she had bumped into Ellen. It was good to have met someone here who she instinctively liked, and who might well become a friend.

'So you think you'll be OK here, Gwen? You have a long stay ahead of you.'

'Oh, yes. I wanted to come to Skye, and the cottage has everything I need. Besides, the location is just perfect. I love being so close to the beach and the sea, and before long I hope to be able to start going up some of the mountains I can see from the window.'

'Well, if you want company,' Ellen said, 'remember me. I'd be happy to come along with you. Just give me a call.'

'Thank you. I will.'

Ellen dug a scrap of paper and a pencil stub out of her jacket pocket. 'This is my phone number and address,' she said, scribbling quickly. 'And when you get into Portree, as I'm sure you will very soon, give me a call then too. We'll have a coffee, or something, and I can show you around. Maybe meet some people.'

'Thanks. I would like that. I'll take you up on your offer — all your offers!'

'Please do.' Ellen finished her coffee, and stretched and yawned. 'Better get going, I suppose. I've got work tomorrow.'

'Before you go, Ellen, I'll just tell you how confused I became when I first arrived. It was quite funny, really. You mentioned Malcolm, the man at the campsite. As I said, he came over here to light the stove, and to show me how everything else works in the cottage. He was really very nice, and helpful.'

'He is. That's Malcolm all over.'

Gwen nodded. 'But what I didn't know, and no-one told me, was that he has a twin brother.'

'Andrew, yes. Ah! I think I can see where you're going with this.'

'I'm sure you can!' Gwen said, laughing. 'The next time I saw Malcolm, he was scarcely speaking. I couldn't understand it. He still helped me, but I wondered what I'd done to offend him.

'Then, on the following occasion, he was friendly and pleasant again, just like the first time. Was it something about me? Or was Malcolm someone with a split personality? It took Mrs McIver to put my mind to rest, but until she told me it never occurred to me that I'd been dealing with two people.'

Ellen chuckled. 'I know what you mean. No-one can tell them apart. Not to look at, anyway. You have to speak to them. Then you can soon tell. Their personalities are totally different.'

'I'll say! They must be our sort of

age. So you'll have known them a long time, I suppose?'

'All my life. We were at school together. They're both good boys, although I have to say I get on better with Malcolm.'

'I think most people would probably say that,' Gwen said ruefully. 'He's certainly a lot easier to talk to.'

'Hands off!' Ellen said, chuckling. 'He's spoken for.'

'I wondered about that.' Gwen laughed, and added, 'What about Andrew?'

'Andrew? Oh, he's all right, basically, but he has problems. He always has had.'

Ellen left soon afterwards, without enlightening Gwen further about the brothers. That was a pity, really, she thought with a sigh. She would have quite liked to hear a little more about them both.

# 12

A couple of days later Gwen got back to work. She felt ready. In fact, she was surprised she had been able to wait so long. She didn't do a lot. But that was not her intention. It was just good to make a start. She knew that, for her, work was the best therapy. Even an hour or two of it could take away a lot of pain.

She didn't work regular hours now, and only ever had done at the very beginning of her career. No nine-to-five for her. That wasn't because she was a precious designer. It was simply that regular hours at a desk or table in an office or design studio, or even at home, didn't suit her. Whenever she had tried that way of working, nothing much had been accomplished. Now she accepted that that was how it was, and how she was. Regular hours didn't lend themselves to her doing her best work.

She was at her best when left to do it her own way. Fortunately, she had found an employer who could tolerate this, and who had even encouraged her in it. The bottom line, of course, was that she had to come up with the goods. The work might be creative, but it was done within the context of a business. Artistry and craft had to pay.

Thankfully, coming up with the goods was something Gwen had always managed to do. Her designs were widely admired in the industry, and her name was well known nationally.

She might not have been in this position had her career followed a different track, but in the past few years she had been working for an old family-owned firm in Leeds that made sure she knew how much she was appreciated. Sometimes she had to smile at how well they looked after her. Working for Fazackerly Brothers was in many ways a dream come true.

Her current predicament provided a good illustration of how well they treated her. James Fazackerly, the older brother, had done everything he possibly could to make sure she felt valued and supported after her accident.

'Take your time, Gwen,' he had advised when he visited her in hospital. 'You've had a terrible experience, and you need to get yourself right. Don't worry about work, or money. Nothing like that. Your job and salary will always be there for you.

'Just think of yourself, and do what you need to do: If there's anything you need that will help, by the way, be sure to let me know. You've been very good for us, and my brother and I are determined you should never want for anything now.'

'That's very kind of you, James,' Gwen said, touched by his obvious sincerity. 'I do appreciate it.'

'When you're better, Gwen, come back to us if you wish — but only if you really want to. If your preference is to say goodbye — perhaps to move on, or to adjust to a different, quieter life

— we would respect that. Absolutely we would. We would deeply regret it, but we wouldn't stand in your way. William and I want only the best for you.'

She had smiled at such a fulsome tribute. It was completely over the top, but she knew it was well meant. The Fazackerly brothers were the latest in a long line of gruff, proud Yorkshire businessmen, but they still wore their hearts on their sleeves.

'Don't be silly, James. Of course I'll come back to work for you. If you will have me, that is. Don't you worry about that! My work is my life, and there's no better place for me to be doing it than at Fazackerly's.'

They had left it there. She had unlimited leave of absence on full pay, and she had all the time she needed to recuperate, and to think about how and where she wanted to live in future. All she needed to do was get herself better. If you had to have a bad accident, she reflected, what better outcome could there be than that?

All this ran through her mind as she began to organise herself to begin work in the cottage on Skye, in the shade of the Black Cuillins, with a breeze rustling the nearby pine trees and the sea whispering not far away. She had no idea what she would do. Basically, she just wanted to sit at a drawing board again. She wanted to hold pen and pencil, and see what happened on the paper in front of her.

Too much time had been spent on computers in recent years. That was inevitable, the way things were in the industry. But her best work had always started with ideas sketched on paper, and that was what she had always liked best. Now seemed a good time to indulge herself. No commitments, nothing that needed finishing to meet a deadline. Just the opportunity to let her imagination play free with whatever her eyes had seen around her.

So she drew. She roughed out patterns and worked on mosaics that blended what she had been seeing since she arrived on the island: grass and heather, gorse and stunted pines, cascading streams, the shadows cast by the mountains, little white cottages, sand and mud. And, of course, the sea — the ever-restless, constantly murmuring, shining sea. It would be a real surprise if she couldn't get anything good out of that lot, she thought.

After an hour or two, she dropped her pens and artist's pencils. She stood up, stretched and moved across the room to stand staring out across the bay. Nothing very much had happened on her drawing board, but at least she had made a start. She had sat there for longer than at any other time in the past couple of months, and she had drawn and doodled with pleasure. She felt happy and well-satisfied.

$$\star \quad \star \quad \star$$

Late morning. Time for a little walk before lunch. The sky was gloomy but she knew appearances could be deceptive.

Once outside, it might well look different. Even if it didn't, all that could change in a moment. The weather here came racing across the broad, restless Atlantic. Who could tell what would come next, or when?

Just as she was about to leave the window and look for her boots and jacket, she saw one of the McIver brothers appear at the entrance to the campsite. He was wrestling with something on the ground, something that looked like a pile of old textile material. She frowned and waited. The she smiled as a sheep went scampering away. Perhaps it had been caught up in the fence, or managed to get itself upside-down. A rescue, anyway.

And who was the rescuer? Impossible to tell. She was no better at distinguishing between the brothers now than she had been the day she arrived. With a chuckle, she went to get ready.

# 13

She was washing up after breakfast when the phone rang She paused and stared at it with surprise. Who could that be? Nobody knew she was here. Then she gave a wry smile. Nobody, that was, but Mrs McIver, her two sons, Mum, Ellen . . . and who knew who else! There was no such thing as being in remote retreat any more.

'Hello?'

'Gwen?'

'Yes, it is. Oh! Hello, Rob.'

She pulled a face. At that moment, Rob was the last person she wanted or expected to hear from.

'How are you, Gwen?'

'OK, thanks. How did you get my phone number?'

'From your mother. I rang her when I didn't hear from you. You said you would let me know where you were.'

'Rob, I've only been here a few days! I haven't had time to think about anything but essentials.'

'Well, your mother knows where you are.'

She let a silence develop before saying gently, 'She's my mother, Rob. Of course she knows where I am.'

'I was worried about . . . '

'Look, Rob. You've caught me at a bad time. Can I call you back?'

'Yes, of course. When will . . . ?'

She pressed the button that ended the call and laid the phone down. Then she stood looking at it for a moment.

Her own phone, her mobile, didn't work here. No reception at all. Not one single bar. So the landline was a very good thing to have. Without it, there would be no communication with the outside world.

She reached to the wall socket and pulled out the BT line. That would have to do for now. She had a lot to think about, and a lot she didn't want to think about.

Later that morning she went out to walk along to the mountain rescue centre and back, one of her customary short walks. Two miles, she reckoned. Admittedly on the flat, but it was still two miles. She could do that comfortably now. Her leg was responding well to the daily exercise. The muscles were getting stronger, and holding the pain at bay. Soon, she thought, glancing across at Sgurr Alasdair! One day, anyway. Hopefully. She was beginning to feel the mountains wouldn't always be beyond her.

Her mood was lifted when she saw new lambs in a field close to Glen Brittle House. An older man from the farm was leaning against the stone wall, watching them.

They exchanged greetings and Gwen said, 'They weren't here last time I was along this road. When did they arrive?'

'Just a few hours ago,' the man said with a grin. 'These are the first, but there should be a good few more by the end of the week.'

He looked tired but happy, which wasn't at all surprising.

'They were born overnight, were they? And you were waiting for them?'

'Aye.' He pushed himself upright and fingered his back gently. 'You have to be there when the time comes, in case there's problems.'

Gwen nodded. She could understand that.

'It's been a long night, then?'

'You're right. It has. But I wouldnae have wanted to miss it.'

It was said with affection. They were all the same, hill sheep farmers, Gwen thought as she moved on. It didn't matter whether they were in Yorkshire or the Scottish highlands and islands. They were still shepherds at heart, watching over their flocks. The quad bikes that so many of them had now, and all the other marvels of modern technology, hadn't altered that.

It was the same with her rugs.

Computers and machines had transformed the industry, but she still felt akin to the ancient people who had sat on the stony ground, working the wool with their fingers — and who, in places, still did that today. Her designs were in that tradition, and so were the images and materials she used. The fruits of the earth. She wouldn't ever want to lose that connection. It was part of the reason why she was here in Glenbrittle: as good a place as any to renew her vows to her craft.

★  ★  ★

She called in at the campsite shop to buy some milk on her way back to the cottage, and there she saw Fiona again. She was playing on a swing dangling from the branch of a stunted pine tree nearby. The little girl waved happily to her as she left the shop, and Gwen smiled and waved back. She really was such a lovely little thing. It was a joy to see her.

A woman she had seen working around the campsite came towards her, carrying bucket and mop, heading for the washrooms. She glanced round to see who Gwen was waving at and came on, smiling.

'Hello!' she said. 'Lovely day.'

'It is,' Gwen assured her. 'Is that your little girl over there on the swing?'

The woman glanced round again and shook her head. 'Fiona? No, she's Andrew's daughter.'

With that, she pushed open the door to the washrooms and disappeared inside.

Then Malcolm intercepted her as she neared the cottage. She knew it was him, rather than Andrew, by his cheerful demeanour. Perhaps, she thought, that would always be the best way to tell them apart.

'Gwen! I was just looking for you.'

'Hi, Malcolm. What's up?'

'Just a message from Ellen. Apparently your phone's not working. She wanted me to ask if you would join us and a few friends tonight for a meal and a drink in Portree.'

'Oh! That's very kind of you both. I would love to.'

'Good. You can travel with me, if that's OK with you?'

'Well . . . ' How to put this? she wondered. 'Will you be drinking — alcohol, I mean?'

Malcolm shook his head. 'Not me, no. You don't need to worry about that. It's my turn to have a sober evening. You and Ellen can both get drunk as lords — or ladies, I should say.'

Gwen laughed. 'I can't see that happening; not a fit, healthy person like Ellen, anyway.'

'What about you?'

She shook her head. 'Me neither. I can hardly walk as it is these days. I might have a glass of wine, but one will be my limit.'

'It could be a very boring evening,' Malcolm said with a frown.

'Dis-invite me, then!' she challenged. 'You don't have to take me.'

He shook his head. 'More than my life's worth. Ellen is more eager to see you than me, I think.'

'Oh, I don't believe that for one moment,' Gwen said with an arch smile.

Malcolm shrugged and grinned.

'You two are an item, I gather?'

'Pretty much. We've known each other all our lives, and we've been going out properly together for a year or two. How about you? Single, or . . . ?'

'Me? Oh, I'm a single girl,' she said without thought. 'Definitely.'

'A career girl, too?'

'Pretty much.'

Malcolm nodded, as if to say he'd thought as much. Then he glanced at his watch and added, 'I'll pick you up about six-thirty, if that's OK?'

'That's fine. Thank you, Malcolm.'

Afterwards, she wondered why she had been so free with information about herself. And had she been quite truthful about her status? Yes, she decided. She had. Rob was in her past. She could see no place for him in her future.

# 14

Portree, or *Portrigh* as the Gaelic sign at the entrance had it, looked a lovely little town, built around an inlet from the sea. The sheltered harbour contained lots of small boats, many of them pleasure craft but quite a few piled high with fishing gear.

'Is it a fishing town?' Gwen asked as they drove down to the quayside.

'Originally, it probably was. But it will always have been a commercial and administrative centre, as well. It had a governor at one time who lived in the castle over there.'

'Appointed by the government in London?'

Malcolm grinned. 'Probably. Somebody had to stop the fighting. It won't always have been peace and harmony on Skye, whatever the tourist promotion people like to pretend. If we couldn't fight the English, we'd have been fighting each other, I expect.'

'Like Leeds on a Friday night, then?'

Malcolm laughed. 'And a lot of other places. The way of the world! Here we are,' he added.

'Is this where Ellen lives?'

'It is now. She used to live at home with her parents, but she got her own place a year or two ago.'

It was a small block of flats just off the quayside. An interesting location to live, Gwen thought. More so than in the rather sedate town centre, probably. There would always be things going on down here. As well as activities connected with the boats, there were a few restaurants and cafés. Even a couple of fish-and-chip shops. How nice, she thought with a wry smile. How civilized!

Malcolm parked in a bay reserved for visitors and went off to collect Ellen.

They started off with a glass of wine in a little bar overlooking the harbour. Ellen was in good form, as was

Malcolm. They made a fine couple, Gwen thought. How well they complemented each other. Ellen quiet and serious; Malcolm a lively spirit. Of course, they had known each other all their lives. That must help. No surprises — no unpleasant surprises, at least, she thought ruefully, with Rob in mind. She envied them.

She was pleased they hadn't thought to bring a spare man to make up a quartet. She hated it when that happened. Having to make conversation with someone she didn't know, and with whom she had nothing in common, did not make for an enjoyable evening in her estimation.

'Are you settled in now at the cottage?' Ellen asked.

'Pretty well, thanks, with the help of the McIver family. And I'm very happy there. It's perfect for me.'

'That's good.'

'Mind you, I would have been stuck without the help of Malcolm from time to time.' She nodded after Malcolm, who had gone to have a quick word with a couple at a nearby table. 'Andrew, too. He's helped me once or twice.'

'Andrew? Oh!'

Ellen seemed surprised, as if she found it hard to believe Andrew could be helpful to anyone.

'I'm getting the hang of distinguishing between them now,' Gwen added with a chuckle. 'When one of them appears, you just have to wait and see if he speaks and smiles.'

'That sums it up perfectly,' Ellen said with satisfaction.

Malcolm returned then with a tray of glasses, and the conversation changed direction.

'You handle that tray very adroitly, Malcolm,' Gwen observed.

Malcolm gave a little bow, deposited the glasses on the table, and gave the tray a spin, making them laugh.

'Oh, stop showing off, Mal!' Ellen protested.

'He's very good, though, isn't he?' Gwen said.

'Well, I should be. I used to do it for a living,' Malcolm told her.

'What? Spin trays?'

'I worked in a cocktail bar.'

'Part-time,' Ellen pointed out.

'Part-time,' Malcolm agreed.

'Where you learned the skills of the trade?'

'Exactly.' He sat down, grinned, and added, 'Before I discovered the joys of the open air in daylight, and became a campsite manager.'

'And owner?'

He shook his head. 'No. The estate owns the land, and the site. I'm just the manager.'

'So it's seasonal work?'

'Pretty much.'

'What do you do in the winter?'

'Ah! That's a bit of a problem. This and that, basically, along with a bit of maintenance on the site. Nothing too demanding.'

'It sounds lovely,' Gwen said, although she wondered if 'this and that' was enough to keep the wolf from the door.

'He's being far too modest,' Ellen said. 'Mal also helps maintain several holiday cottages owned by the family, and helps his mum look after his dad. Mr McIver is bed-ridden now. So Mal has plenty to occupy him. There's always work for him to do.'

'I'm sure there is,' Gwen said, thinking all that probably was enough.

'It's not all down to me, though,' Malcolm said. 'My brother pitches in as well.'

'Your brother?' Ellen sighed and shook her head.

Gwen was beginning to see that Ellen didn't think much of Andrew. She wondered if that caused any friction between the brothers.

'But basically I don't have Ellen's brains, you see,' Malcolm said with a cheerful grin. 'No bank would employ me. So I have to do what I can.'

Ellen swatted him with a menu card and he pulled back, laughing.

'I don't believe you for a moment,' Gwen told him. 'It's more likely a bank wouldn't suit you, not at all. I think you just prefer working in the open air for the summer. And I can't say I blame you.'

He nodded agreement. 'You're right. I wouldn't last five minutes in an indoor job, not in the summer. I'd go crazy.'

'What about your brother? Is he the same as you?'

'Andrew?' Malcolm shrugged. 'Not really, no.'

'What does he do usually? Your mother said he was just helping you out temporarily.'

'Oh, Andrew's a highly skilled man. He's got plenty of brains as well.'

'So he's just helping while you're busy getting set up for the season?'

Malcolm nodded, but looked uncomfortable with the question. It seemed time for a change of subject.

'Andrew is a fine craftsman,' Ellen interjected, coming to the rescue. 'I won't deny that. He designs and builds the most beautiful wooden staircases, usually in oak.'

'Really?' Gwen's eyebrows shot upwards with astonishment. 'Staircases?

Ellen nodded.

'Not now, though,' Malcolm said. 'He doesn't now.'

'Not at the moment,' Ellen agreed.

Gwen looked from one to the other of them. 'That's amazing,' she said. 'I didn't know there were people who specialized like that, but when you think about it . . . '

'What about you?' Ellen interrupted. 'Tell us about yourself.'

It seemed as if neither of them wanted to talk any more about Andrew, which wasn't unreasonable. Not entirely. They were looking to have a fun night out, after all, not a discussion about a family member they had known all their lives and didn't find particularly entertaining.

All the same, Gwen thought, what Ellen had said was very interesting. And whatever could Malcolm have meant? Why didn't Andrew do it now? Was he simply 'between things', as the old saying went, and having a rest?

There was also Fiona to wonder about. How did she fit into Andrew's life? And what of Fiona's mother? There had been no mention of her yet.

She could see she would have to talk to Ellen, or to Malcolm, another time about the rather mysterious Andrew. That is, if it wouldn't be trespassing on ground upon which neither of them wished to tread.

So, instead of questioning them further about Andrew, she told them a little about her career with Fazackerly Brothers, and what she hoped to do in the next few months.

'How interesting,' Ellen said with admiration. 'You must be a very creative person, Gwen.'

'Oh, no! I don't think of myself like that at all. I'm a craftsman, basically.'

'But you must be creative?'

Gwen shrugged. 'A bit, perhaps.'

She was uncomfortable with the way the discussion was going. She preferred to talk about her work rather than herself. Thankfully, Ellen let her off the hook.

'But first you want to strengthen your leg, and get yourself fit again?'

'You're right,' Gwen admitted ruefully. 'That has to come first.'

Malcolm looked interested. 'You had an accident, Ellen said?'

'Car crash,' she admitted. 'A bad one. The driver was drunk, unfortunately. It wasn't me, by the way. I was just a passenger who got a lift with the wrong person.'

'No man in your life to drive you home?'

She paused before saying, 'There used to be. But he was the driver.'

'Ah!' Malcolm fell quiet.

Ellen finished off her wine, pushed her chair back and said, 'Come on! Let's go and get something to eat. I'm starving.'

# 15

They joined four other people at an Italian restaurant in the town centre, people who were obviously good friends of Ellen and Malcolm. It was hard to tell if they were couples or a group of singletons. Gwen pondered the question for a moment and then stopped. It really didn't matter either way. It was just that she was used to socialising with other couples as part of a couple. Habit. Custom, at least. She still hadn't got used to not being with Rob. That was going to take time.

It was a typical Italian, and they had a lot of fun ordering a variety of meals between them. 'Cheap and cheerful' might have been an unfair comment for such a pleasant, friendly place, but it seemed appropriate. The waiters went out of their way to ensure their customers enjoyed their evening.

'It's always the same here,' confided Liz, one of the women in the group.

'How?' Gwen asked. 'A party, you mean?'

'Exactly!' Liz giggled. 'Every time. No wonder we come so often.'

The group was too big and noisy, as was the restaurant itself, for a many-handed sensible conversation. People either shouted across the table or spoke more quietly to a near neighbour. For a time, Liz engaged Gwen's attention.

'You're from Yorkshire?' she asked. 'At least, that's what I think Ellen said.'

'Yes, I am. I work in Leeds, and live just outside — near Otley, if you know it?'

'Slightly. I once had a boyfriend from around there. He lived in Ilkley.'

'Oh, that's not far away. How about yourself? Are you Skye-born, like Ellen?'

'Oh, yes. We all are.'

'Don't tell me you went to school together, like Ellen and Malcolm?'

'We did! How did you know?' Liz

laughed. 'Us here, and Andrew of course, we all went through school together. That's Malcolm's brother, by the way. Have you met him?'

Gwen nodded. 'Once or twice, yes.'

'How did you get on with him?'

'Fine, I think'

'That's good. He doesn't get on with everyone. He never did, even as a young boy.'

'Oh?'

'He would soon lose patience with anyone less clever than him — like me! That's the top and bottom of it, really. Least, I think so. No wonder he suffers from depression now.'

'Does he? I didn't realise. I just thought he was very quiet.'

'Oh, he is quiet! If he's ever spoken to you, you're one of the lucky ones — or the unlucky ones. Nice man, though,' Liz concluded, rather improbably. 'At least, he was until that wife of his left him.'

High spirits around the table intervened before Gwen could ask Liz what on earth she had meant. The evening rolled on, as did the several conversations. Then Malcolm got to his feet, glass in hand, and invited everyone to drink a toast to their guest from afar. It could have been excruciatingly embarrassing for Gwen, being made the reluctant centre of attention, but somehow it wasn't. She had been made so welcome that she was relaxed and happy to respond.

'Gwen's not been here long,' Malcolm said portentously, 'but already she fits Glenbrittle like a glove.'

'The other way round, Malcolm,' another of the men, Denny, said.

'What?'

'Glenbrittle fits her like a glove, you ignoramus!'

'Oh, yes. I see what you mean. Anyway,' Malcolm added, grinning at Gwen, 'you're very welcome here!'

'Thank you, Malcolm.' Gwen smiled and said, 'I didn't know we were going to have speeches, and I haven't prepared one. So I'm not going to try to make a speech. I'll just say thank you to everyone for such an enjoyable evening, and for making me feel so welcome.'

That earned her a round of applause. People were more than ready to find something to be happy about, it seemed. And so a lovely evening drew to a close.

Later, Gwen rather regretted not having been able to ask Liz more about Andrew, but she decided it had probably been for the best. Andrew's circumstances were none of her business, even if she was curious. It wouldn't do to go burrowing into the life of someone who was such a stranger.

Still, she had learned something more about him during the course of the evening, hopefully enough to prevent her making any terrible social blunders when next she came across him or Fiona.

# 16

It was when she was walking around the bay towards the headland that she next saw Andrew — the mysterious, enigmatic, difficult-sounding Andrew.

At the time she was feeling very pleased with herself. Now she could walk a couple of miles without a significant problem. She knew that because she had a little GPS device that told her exactly how far she had gone. It even showed her diagrammatically where her perambulation had taken her — not that she needed that. The capability of the device was way in excess of what she wanted, needed, or was interested in. She just wanted to know how far she had walked when she went out on her daily venture.

Glancing at the screen, she could see that she had covered 1.75 miles. So, in a quarter of an hour, she would have done exactly two miles. She knew that because she had done this walk before, and measured it a couple of times already.

'You're doing much better,' she heard someone call.

She spun round. No-one was behind or in front of her. Her head turned sideways and then she saw him, a little way uphill from where she stood. But which of them was it? She took a chance.

'Hello, Andrew! I didn't notice you.'

He had been standing still. Now he set off in a vigorous, sliding gait that brought him quickly down the steep slope to where she stood.

'Hello,' he said with the suggestion of a smile.

She smiled back, thinking that this was a surprise in more ways than one. 'Where have you come from?'

He nodded over his shoulder. 'I've just been up to Coire Lagan.'

'Really? How lovely.'

He nodded, looking surprised that

she seemed to know where he meant.

'I study the map,' she said shyly. 'One day I hope to get up there myself.'

'You will,' he said.

It was such a serious, straightforward comment that she believed he meant it. She felt quite uplifted. 'You think?'

He nodded again. 'I've seen it before. How to recover from an injury. You're doing the right things, and it's going well. I can see that.'

'Oh? Have you been watching me?' she asked archly, without thinking. 'I'm just joking,' she added quickly as his expression hardened.

'No, not really. See you,' he said, turning to walk away.

'Wait!' she called a little desperately.

He stopped and looked back at her. 'What?'

'How long would it take to get up there? To Coire Lagan, I mean.'

'You, or me?'

'Ah! That's a point. You, then.'

'Two hours.'

'And longer for me?'

'Of course. At the moment,' he added. 'When you're fully fit, it will be a different story.'

He gave her a little wave and walked off, heading down to the campsite.

Such a difficult person, she thought sadly as she continued on her own way. So prickly and remote. She could see why he had such a poor reputation.

Yet there was something about him: a nice guy struggling to get out, perhaps. She wondered if he was just shy. In itself, that could explain a lot.

Fiona came to mind then. Such a lovely little girl. And Andrew looked after her himself, it seemed, since the departure of his wife. It must be a challenge. He would have his hands full. That was another thing. How had it come about? she wondered. It was pretty unusual for a mother to leave a child behind when she left her husband.

She shrugged. Too many questions. It was nothing to do with her, she reminded herself. It was just that this small place was a bit of a goldfish bowl.

You saw people every day, and inevitably you wondered about them. Sheer nosiness? Probably, she thought with a rueful smile.

* * *

All thoughts of Andrew were soon forgotten once she got back to the cottage. She hadn't been through the door five minutes when the phone rang, the strange sound reverberating through the building as if it had been calibrated to serve people who were quite deaf. She rather regretted having reinstalled it.

'Hello?'

'It's me, Gwen. You said you would call me back.'

She grimaced. 'Sorry, Rob. I did, didn't I? It's just that I've been so busy here, sorting things out, trying to get down to some work, and . . . oh, I don't know! One thing and another. How are you, anyway?'

'OK. Missing you. But managing all right. Wondering what we're going to be doing, of course. You and me, I mean.'

'It's difficult, isn't it?'

'Well . . . Not really. I mean, I understood when you said you needed some time to yourself after all that had happened. You came out of the accident badly. And it was my fault. We both know that. So I understood, but . . . '

'But?'

'Well, I feel I'm in limbo. I can't be doing this much longer. Can't we get together, and sort things out?'

She paused a moment, collecting her thoughts. Perhaps this was the moment she had been subconsciously awaiting.

'You want to know where we stand, you and I? Do we have a future together? That's what you mean, Rob, isn't it?'

'Well, yes. It is. You can't blame me. I mean, yes, you can blame me for the accident. Even I blame me! But I have a life to lead, as well as you. I need to know what you want to do. So what do you think?'

'You should get on with your life,

Rob. That's what I think. The accident did change things for me, but only in the sense that it brought me to a conclusion more quickly than might have happened otherwise.

'It's over, Rob. We had some good times together, but I don't want to continue with the relationship.'

After a long pause, he said, 'Does that mean there's someone else?'

'No, Rob. It doesn't. There isn't anyone else, but I know now that you and I are not meant to be together. That's all. Better to admit it now than take forever realising it.'

'That's how you feel?'

'It is.'

'Well, it's not how I feel, but . . . OK, then,' he said. 'If that's what you want?'

'It is. I'm starting a new life, a different life. You should do the same.'

'You're right. I will.'

'Just one more thing, Rob. I don't blame you for the accident. It could have happened at any time, to anyone. So please don't blame yourself too harshly.'

'Nice of you to say so, Gwen. I appreciate it.'

'Take care — and good luck!'

'You, too.'

That was that. It was over. She felt nothing but relief.

★   ★   ★

Afterwards, she thought she had let him down gently. She did blame him for the accident. Of course she did. He'd been drunk, and still driving. Not for the first time, either. There was no-one else but him to blame — except herself for being with him at the time. She still hadn't worked out why she had let him drive her home after the party, instead of phoning for a taxi. Fatigue and weakness, presumably. Well, she'd paid the price for that — and how!

But it was over now. She was glad they wouldn't have to perpetuate the myth that it was just a temporary separation while she convalesced. All the same, she shed a tear or two for

Rob, and for them both together, and for what might have been. She couldn't help it. But it was over, she ended up repeating firmly to herself. That was it. Move on.

# 17

Increasingly, Fiona puzzled Gwen. The more she saw of her, the more something didn't seem quite right. From her vantage point on the path uphill from the toilet block at the campsite, she could see Fiona quite clearly at the moment, and once again there was something odd about how she behaved. She couldn't put her finger on it, as her mum might have said, but something was making her uneasy. It wasn't the first time she had thought that, either.

Fiona was sitting on a wooden box, surveying the world of the campsite before her. And what a strange world it was for a little girl her age. Some might think it idyllic, but it wasn't. Not really. Not for a little girl. For a start, there were no other children around. There would be later in the summer, presumably, but there were none now. Other children Fiona's age were all still in school, the summer holidays far too distant a prospect for them even to be dreaming about.

Nor would there have been any other children here throughout the winter, either. Perhaps that was why Fiona seemed a little odd? She didn't have any playmates. So she wasn't playing, which was what you would expect young children to be doing.

So why wasn't she at school, with other children? This was a pretty remote place, it was true, but didn't all children go to school? In fact, wasn't it even a legal requirement for children to attend school? So why wasn't Fiona there?

It was a mystery.

Gwen recalled then that when she had first spoken to Fiona, the little girl had asked about her bad leg, and then confided that her own leg was better now too. Perhaps that had something to do with her not being at school? Perhaps she too had been convalescing?

If Fiona had been hurt in some way — an accident, perhaps — that could explain why she had taken notice of someone else who was limping. Something in common? A fellow casualty? Comrade in arms?

Gwen gave a wry smile. Speculation. But it was possible. She would have to make some discreet inquiries.

She found herself wondering again why Fiona didn't seem to play at all. Even if she didn't have any playmates, she should still be playing at, or with, something. Children all had dolls and model soldiers, toy pets and favourite hidey-holes. Even isolated, lonely children found ways to amuse themselves, one way or another. They could always invent imaginary playmates if they didn't have any real ones. But this little girl didn't seem to do any of that.

Mind you, Gwen thought with amusement, even if Fiona didn't play with people or things, she did seem to find ways of entertaining herself. Look at her now! Observation seemed to be her thing. There she was, sitting like a little old lady, keeping an eye on everyone and everything around the campsite. Perhaps she was just by nature a spectator, rather than a player. How would that work out in the long run, though? Problems? Possibly. But she just didn't know enough about children to be sure.

Stop it! It's not your business, she told herself firmly. She got up and resumed her walk back to the cottage. Fiona was probably fine. She was just different, and since when was being different a matter for concern? She shouldn't worry about her. Just leave her father, and the rest of the McIver family, to do that.

\* \* \*

Back at the cottage, she made a mug of coffee and took it to her work station, where she doodled on a sheet of paper for a while. The subsequent pattern, she photographed and transferred onto her laptop to join all the other ideas she had developed. It was quite a collection she was assembling. She hoped George, Head of Design back at Fazackerly's, would be pleased when she got round to sending him something.

Then she yawned, feeling vaguely dissatisfied, and got up to go and stand by the window. Despite her best efforts, she wasn't really very excited about what she had produced so far. She had returned to her work that morning full of eagerness and intent, and she had got something new down on paper, but it hadn't matched the promise she had felt on the hillside.

What she had certainly wasn't rubbish. Some of it would be welcomed back at Fazackerly's, she was sure. But? Well, perhaps the word she sought was 'inspired'. What she had produced was not exactly inspired. It was just . . . well, professional, and OK. That was the only way she could describe it. She felt a bit deflated.

Why was that? she wondered. Well,

she had come here determined to capture the spirit of the place — the colours and textures of the heather and the sky and the sea and the mountains, all of that — and to an extent she had, but not to a sufficient extent. She just wasn't thrilled when she looked at what she'd got. She didn't know why, either, or what she could do about it.

Perhaps she had come to the wrong place? Perhaps Glenbrittle wasn't where she should be?

Oh, no! She flatly rejected that idea. It was wonderful here. She just hadn't caught the essence of the place yet. But there was nowhere else on earth she would rather be. Of that, she was certain.

She would get it eventually, she hoped. Perhaps. And if she didn't? Move on? She shook her head. Not that. But she didn't know what else she could do right now. She would have to cross that bridge when she came to it.

# 18

'How far have we walked today?' Ellen asked mischievously.

Gwen made an elaborate play of studying her GPS and then announced the precise answer: 'Five point seven eight miles.'

'Goodness! As far as that? We are doing well.'

'Well, I am. It wasn't much of a walk for you, I'm afraid.'

Nonsense!' Ellen said crisply. 'It was a lovely walk. You don't have to do a marathon every time you go out, you know. That's not the idea at all. Anyway, I'm so happy for you, Gwen. Being able to walk that far again must make coming here seem justified.'

Gwen nodded agreement as they neared the cottage. It was true. She was well pleased. Now she could walk that distance without significant discomfort.

When she came here, she hadn't been able to do it at all. Simple as that.

The weekly walk she had started doing with Ellen had been a big help, but most of her walking had been done alone. Day after day she had trod the rugged paths around the cottage, her muscles strengthening with every outing.

'What about your work?' Ellen asked. 'Is that going well, too?'

'Oh, all right, I suppose. But I've not done anything terribly special yet.'

'That will happen,' Ellen said firmly. 'You're too impatient. How long have you been here, after all? A month? Six weeks?'

'Going on seven weeks, actually. But yes, you're probably right. I am impatient. It's like with the walking. I'm OK on the flat, but the mountains are still out of reach.'

'In time, my girl! Give it time. You can't expect to be like Andrew already.'

'Oh? Is he a mountain man?'

Ellen nodded. 'A very good one, actually. Walker, rock-climber, general

123

mountaineer — he's an all-round type. I'm just a walker.'

'And that's what I would like to be. What about Malcolm? Is he a climber, too?'

'No.' Ellen shook her head. 'I think he did some when he was a boy, but he's not interested now. In fact, he doesn't do much of anything now except work. Sometimes I get worried about him. But he doesn't take any notice when I tell him he needs a hobby, or a recreation.'

'Maybe it's easier for him in the winter?'

'Yes, it is. The summer season is his busy time.'

'Mountaineering, then. So that's another way Malcolm is different to Andrew. At last I'm starting to see them as separate people, each with his own identity.'

'You'd better believe it!'

As was their custom after these walks, they prepared a light lunch together and opened a bottle of elderflower water. Then they sat down at the kitchen table.

'I'm starving,' Ellen announced, 'and this tuna salad looks so good.'

'You're right. Dig in! Thinking of Andrew,' Gwen mused, 'you never did tell me what happened with his wife.'

'Well, there's not a lot to say. She left. That's about all I know.'

'How long had they been married?'

'A year? Not much more. Andrew met her on a job he was doing in Aberdeen, and brought her back with him. Then they got married.' Ellen grimaced and continued, 'I never liked her. She was odd.'

'In what way?'

'Well, I thought she was flaky. You know what I mean? Full of herself. Self-obsessed. Inconsistent. Bouncing around from one thing to another when it came to jobs. Five minutes in the supermarket in Broadford, then a bar in Portree for a while. Claimed to be a writer, but I don't think she ever did any writing.'

'A writer? What sort of writer?'

'Poet, or so Malcolm said.' Ellen thought for a moment and then added, 'Does that count? Poetry?'

'As writing?' Gwen screwed up her face in thought. 'Poetry? I suppose so. Not many words to the pound, though, are there?'

Ellen laughed aloud heartily. That was another thing Gwen liked about her. She had a good sense of humour, and wasn't afraid to show it.

When she had finished laughing, Ellen said, ' 'Katarina the Poet', me and Malcolm used to call her.'

'Katarina, eh? So Malcolm didn't like her either?'

Ellen shook her head. 'Malcolm couldn't stand her — and that's saying something. Malcolm likes everybody.'

'Except Katarina.'

'Except her.'

'Well, Andrew must have liked her.'

'Yes — for a time, I expect he did. I'll make a pot of tea now, shall I?' Ellen added.

'Please. If you don't mind.'

That was yet another good thing about Ellen, Gwen reflected. She was such a very thoughtful person. She knew Gwen would be more tired than she was after the walk. So she had volunteered to make the tea.

'Where does Fiona come into it?' Gwen asked when Ellen sat down again. 'Why didn't she go with her mother? That's what usually happens, isn't it?'

'Her mother? Oh, I see what you mean. But Katarina isn't Fiona's mother.'

'No?'

Ellen shook her head. 'Oh, no. Fiona was around long before Katarina turned up.'

# 19

'Ellen, stop being such a tease! You really are very enigmatic.'

'I don't know what you mean, I'm sure.'

'Deliberately obtuse. Tantalising. Will that do?'

Wearing a smug smile, Ellen sat down again. 'Haven't I ever told you about Fiona's mother?'

'No, you have not. Tell me now, please.'

'Well, it was some girl he met at university who didn't want a baby, or an abortion either. I don't even know her name. She disappeared soon after Fiona was born. Just walked out and disappeared.'

Ellen shrugged and added, 'That's all I know, really. It's all Malcolm knows, as well.'

Gwen was shocked. 'She just abandoned her baby? That's terrible!'

'Welcome to the real world, Gwen. You must have led a very sheltered life. Oh, I'm sorry! I didn't mean that.'

'Yes, you did. And you're right. These things do happen, I know that. Leeds isn't exactly a tranquil backwater. It's just that I don't personally know people who have done anything like that.'

And she was truly shocked by what Ellen had told her. Somehow it was different when real people, people you knew, were involved, rather than people you read about in a newspaper, or heard about on television or the radio.

'Poor Andrew,' she murmured. 'He hasn't had much luck with women, has he?'

Ellen shook her head and yawned. 'In some ways,' she added reflectively, 'what happened isn't too surprising. Andrew has always been difficult, and any woman who gets involved with him has to be too.'

'What are you saying, Ellen? The woman was leaving Andrew behind, as much as her baby?'

Ellen nodded. 'Unwanted baggage, both. She must have had enough of him, and didn't fancy staying for his child either. Horrible, I know, but . . . it happened.'

Gwen thought about what Ellen had said. 'Perhaps there's nothing wrong with Andrew,' she suggested. 'Maybe he just keeps on finding the wrong women?'

Ellen smiled. 'Like a serial offender, you mean?'

Gwen chuckled reluctantly. 'Exactly! He keeps on doing the same thing, with the same result. I believe it was Einstein who said that was the definition of madness: keeping on doing the same thing over and over, and expecting the outcome to be different.'

Ellen yawned. 'I don't know about that. Anyway, I'm tired of thinking and talking about Andrew.'

'Well, what about Fiona? Let's talk about her. She's a lovely little girl, but so strange and sad-seeming. Now I can see why.'

'She certainly hasn't had it easy,' Ellen admitted. 'And you're right. She is a sweet little thing. I have to admit, Andrew has done very well with her. After all, he's brought her up by himself. Mrs McIver wanted to look after her, but Andrew wouldn't hear of it.'

'A single parent who's a man? That's still pretty unusual, isn't it?'

Ellen nodded. 'I suppose Andrew has his good points.'

Perhaps more than he was being given credit for, Gwen thought.

'Oh, I know what I meant to ask you, Ellen. Why doesn't Fiona go to school?'

'Malcolm says Andrew has some sort of agreement that he can do home tuition with her. From time to time, people check to make sure it's actually happening, but essentially Andrew is educating her himself.'

'That's amazing.'

'And difficult. It couldn't happen without his family supporting him. Malcolm and his parents do an awful lot to help.'

131

'How has that arrangement come about?'

Ellen shrugged. 'I'm not really sure. There were some problems with Fiona. She was ill, I think, but I don't know what with. Anyway, it was thought this was the best way of dealing with things.'

Gwen nodded, thinking it made sense. She wondered what had been wrong with Fiona. Something serious, it sounded like.

'Where do they actually live?'

'Andrew and Fiona? At the moment, in that cottage next to the campsite.'

'Behind the static caravans?'

'That's right. The caravans are for the staff — including Malcolm — during the season, but Andrew rents the cottage.'

'That's handy.'

Ellen nodded.

'During the summer there'll be plenty of children on the campsite for Fiona to play with,' Gwen said thoughtfully. 'Not in the winter, though.'

'No.' Ellen yawned again. 'I'm tired.

I'd better get going. I have some shopping to do in Portree before I go back to work tomorrow.'

'Of course. I forget you're not a lady of leisure.'

'Like you, you mean? How I wish!'

As she was leaving, Ellen suddenly turned very serious and said, 'Don't get too interested in Andrew, Gwen.'

'Whatever do you mean?'

'Just that. He would bring you nothing but pain and heartache. I've seen it before. You have a good life. Don't put it all at risk.'

# 20

'Is this your garden?' a voice asked.

Gwen spun round from the rose bush she was inspecting. 'Oh hello, Fiona! I didn't hear you coming. What are you up to?'

'Nothing, really. Is this your house? Are you doing the garden?'

'It's my house for now, Fiona — for the summer, that is.'

'And you're gardening?'

'Yes. Well . . . I'm just doing a little bit of tidying up. That's all. I was just admiring these roses. Aren't they pretty?'

She pointed to the rambler that was starting to flower on the south side of the garden shed, where it was protected from the usual winds as well as getting all the sun going. Fiona agreed that the roses were pretty, but without a lot of enthusiasm. Flowers didn't seem to be her thing.

'We have lots of flowers in our garden,' she offered. 'Daddy looks after them. Sometimes I help him.'

'That's good, Fiona. He'll need your help, I should think.'

The little girl nodded, as if the point was obvious. 'I could help you?' she suggested.

'Have you got time? Won't your daddy wonder where you are?'

'He knows.'

'Oh?'

Had Fiona told him she was coming here? How odd. How odd for her to *be* here, even.

'Have you got a little girl like me?' Fiona asked.

Gwen smiled and shook her head. 'No, I'm not so lucky as your daddy.'

Fiona absorbed that information with quiet dignity, as if she knew how lucky her father was to have her. She really was a remarkably self-possessed little thing, Gwen thought, much amused.

'Is your leg better now?' was the next question, one that had been asked before.

'Much, much better, thank you. I can walk quite a long way now.'

'I've seen you. Daddy has, too. You walk around by the sea every day.'

'I do, yes. At least, I try to. The exercise strengthens my leg.'

'Soon will you be able to climb the mountains, like Daddy?'

'Oh, I don't know about that! That might be a step too far for me. Do you go into the mountains with Daddy?'

'Sometimes. If I feel like it. But it's hard. It hurts.'

'I bet it does!' Taking a leap, Gwen said, 'What about your leg, Fiona?'

The little girl shrugged. 'Sometimes it hurts. They both do.'

So she'd been right, Gwen thought. She has had a leg problem, which probably is why she took an interest in me and my leg.

'Can I see inside your house?'

Where had that come from? Gwen wondered with even more amusement. Was that behind the purpose of Fiona's visit? Had she exhausted all other points of interest in the vicinity of the campsite, and wanted to see somewhere new?

'Tell you what, Fiona. I was just going to do some dead-heading on the roses — cut off the dead flowers. If you could help me for a bit, afterwards we could go inside and have some hot chocolate and a biscuit. How does that sound?'

Fiona considered the proposal carefully before committing. 'Yes,' she finally announced. 'I will help you with the dead flowers.'

\* \* \*

Gwen swept her worksheets to one side and they sat at the kitchen table together, sipping mugs of hot chocolate. Fiona seemed quite at ease, her eyes giving the room a quick, initial sweep and then returning to the kitchen table.

'I like to draw,' she confided, studying Gwen's equipment.

'Do you? Anything in particular?'

'Children, and mummies and daddies mostly. What do you like drawing?'

'Oh, hills and heather, sheep, the sea. Things like that.'

'I see,' Fiona said gravely, nodding like a little wise old woman.

'How old are you, Fiona?'

'Six, now.'

'Now?'

'I used to be five. For a long time I was. Now I'm six.'

'So have you had a birthday recently?'

Fiona nodded. 'On April the twentieth.'

'Really? I'm so sorry I missed it. Did you have a party?' she asked, unthinkingly.

The little girl shook her head. Gwen winced. How could she, without other children? How clumsy of her!

'It will be better for you in the summer, Fiona. There'll be lots of children on the campsite then.'

'Like last year?'

'Yes. I'm sure there will be. It's just

that most children are in school now, and . . . Well, it's still too cold for camping for most people.'

School, she thought, wincing. There again she had stumbled unthinkingly into a thicket of difficulty. She really would have to be more careful. She didn't want to upset her.

But talking to Fiona was like negotiating a minefield. At least she hadn't said too much about mothers — yet!

'One day I'll go to school, Daddy said.'

'Yes, I expect you will. In Portree, perhaps?'

Fiona nodded but looked a bit uncertain — unsure, perhaps, where or what Portree was. It was such a lonely, remote life for her here, Gwen thought once again. However well Andrew strived to care for her and see to her education, that was still true.

'I don't have a mummy,' Fiona said next, almost as if she could read Gwen's mind. 'There's just me and Daddy.'

'I know that, Fiona,' Gwen said

gently. 'But thank you for telling me.'

Fiona pushed herself away from the table. 'I must go now,' she said. 'Thank you for the hot chocolate. I may come again for some more.'

'Please do!' Gwen said, smiling. 'You're very welcome, Fiona, but be sure to let Daddy know where you are.'

Fiona seemed satisfied in all respects as she left. Points made, perhaps? Curiosity satisfied?

As the little girl gave her a last wave before breaking into a run that would carry her at speed back home, Gwen felt she had been visited by a solemn plenipotentiary, one come from a distant land to see how she lived. She wondered how well she had withstood the scrutiny.

# 21

From the window of the spare bed-room, now her occasional work room, Gwen could usually see Sgurr Alasdair, the highest peak in the Cuillins, for at least part of the day. She couldn't always make it out, but on a clear day there it would be, standing majestically against a pale blue sky like a smaller version of the Matterhorn. It made her shiver, more with pleasure than fear. One day, she kept on promising herself, one day I will get up there.

She had discovered that the peak was named after one of the pioneering mountain men of Skye, Alexander Nicolson, who was the first person known to have climbed it. That had been back in the nineteenth century, in 1873 to be exact. Many had climbed it in the subsequent century and a half, but it still wasn't something to be taken lightly. Gwen knew she would have to be a lot stronger than she was now to get anywhere near the summit of Sgurr Alasdair.

In the meantime, there were other things she would like to try that were a bit less daunting. Climbing up to Coire Lagan was one of them. That was a corrie with a lochan, a small lake, about halfway up to the summit of Alasdair. Ever since she had heard the name fall so magically from Andrew's lips, she had harboured an ambition to see it. Although she had little idea what it would look like, she was sure it would be wonderfully beautiful. '*Coire Lagan,*' she whispered. The very name fascinated her.

She would try to reach it one day soon, she promised herself, turning away from the window. But not quite yet. She still wasn't fit enough for a challenge like that.

She returned to her work table and considered some of the sketches she had made recently. Not bad, she thought. They were improving. Soon she would have material ready to send to Fazackerly's. They had been very good about not bothering her, but they might be starting to wonder what had become of her — and if she was doing any work at all. It would be good to offer them some proof that she wasn't just lying in bed all day.

For the best part of another hour she worked steadily: revising, fine-tuning, nursing the ideas along. Then, just as she was tiring, she was interrupted.

'Hello! Can I come in?' a little voice called timidly.

Gwen smiled and jumped up. She knew who that was. Fiona had visited her once or twice now, and Gwen always enjoyed her appearances.

'What are you doing today?' the little girl asked.

'Some sketching. Drawing. These are ideas for patterns for rugs — you know, little carpets?'

'Like ours?'

'Probably, but I haven't seen yours.'

She showed some of her sketches to Fiona, who seemed quite interested.

'Can I do some drawing?' Fiona asked.

'Yes. Of course you can. Let me make some space for you on the table. Then I'll give you some pencils and a sketching pad.'

They settled down to work together at the big table. Strangely, perhaps, Gwen didn't find her young visitor a nuisance or a distraction. Not at all. She was quite happy to have her there. Apart from anything else, she was a quiet, studious child, and once she got immersed in something it occupied her for some time. So, together, they sketched and drew for a while. It was quite a harmonious little scene, Gwen thought with a smile. Very domestic, even.

'What are you working on, Fiona?' she asked eventually. 'May I see?'

'Yes.'

Fiona sat back and made way for Gwen to stand up and look over her shoulder. There was nothing secretive or possessive about her. She wasn't timid, either. The impression she always gave was that she regarded her work as deserving of respect, and herself as an equal amongst equals. Well, why not? Gwen thought with a smile. What was wrong with that? She found it quite endearing.

'Oh, I see,' she said thoughtfully now, as she studied Fiona's drawing. 'It's your favourite family, isn't it?'

She had seen this family group once or twice before. It was a study Fiona seemed to return to very often, never tiring of it. No doubt that was for very understandable reasons. She seemed to be portraying her notion of the ideal family.

'That's the daddy,' Fiona said now.

'And this one is the mummy?'

'Yes. They have four children.'

'Four! Goodness. That's quite a lot, isn't it?'

'Yes. The children need brothers and sisters to play with, don't they? And each boy needs a brother, and each girl should have a sister.'

'I see.' Gwen nodded. 'That's a good idea. It will mean a lot of work for the mummy, though, won't it?'

'Oh, she won't mind,' Fiona said with a dismissive sniff. 'She's very happy.'

Gwen studied the figures, looking for signs of resemblance to people she knew. There were none that she could see. This was a work of pure imagination, possibly conjured up by memories of family groups Fiona had seen on the campsite during the previous summer.

'Your drawings of people are very good, Fiona.'

'Yes,' the little girl agreed cheerfully. 'They're my best ones, actually.'

Gwen suppressed a little smile. It wouldn't do to appear patronising. This was a child as bright as a button. She couldn't risk offending her.

'And this is the family dog over here?'

'Yes. The cat is outside.'

'So we can't see her at the moment?'

'No. She'll come inside later, when

it's getting cold and she's hungry.'

'I see.'

So Fiona was capable of play, and of conjuring up imaginary people to accompany her. Gwen felt relieved. It meant she wasn't locked away on her own all the time, thinking of nobody but herself. That seemed good.

The representation of the figures was curious. Surprisingly, perhaps, considering the back story Fiona had for each of them, they were not finely detailed. Rather, they were dashed off in the way a cartoonist might have done it. They were representative of an idea rather than portraits of people.

And, just as a cartoonist would have done, Fiona had somehow brought a sense of movement and character into her picture. You couldn't quite make out their faces, but you knew who they were and what they were doing. Gwen wondered how she had done it, and if it was pure accident or if the child had a talent. Hard to say at the moment. But something to watch out for in future.

'It's a lovely picture, Fiona,' Gwen concluded.

'Yes,' her little visitor agreed, again without false modesty. 'It is.'

# 22

She was always so glad to see Malcolm. He was just that kind of person, the type who brightened even the cloudiest day. He was unfailingly friendly and helpful. So it was a welcome change to see him one morning looking like he needed help himself.

'Morning, Malcolm! What's the problem? Can I help?'

He was struggling, trying to fix a small gate that seemed to have come off its hinges.

'Gwen! You're a sight for sore eyes. Could you just ease this gate up for me?'

Gwen did as he asked. She could see it was a two-person job. One was needed to hold the gate in position, while the other held the hinge and screws in place and manipulated the screwdriver.

'You need a third arm, Malcolm. That, or someone to help you.'

'I do. You're right. That no-good brother of mine has disappeared just when I need him. He must have known.'

'Malcolm!' Gwen said, laughing. 'Shame on you. Andrew, avoid work? He wouldn't do any such thing.'

'No, you're right. He works as hard as anyone around here, even if he doesn't get a proper wage.'

'Why's that?'

'Oh, he's just helping out. That's all. He's not on the staff. So I can't pay him what he deserves.'

Gwen's eyebrows went up with surprise. That didn't sound right. 'He works but doesn't get paid?'

'It's complicated,' Malcolm said. 'There! That's one of 'em done.'

He finished with one hinge and moved on to the other.

'This gate gets a terrible lot of abuse, you know. I'm always mending it. People swing it too hard after them. I hear it from the caravan, banging against the post. It's a busy footpath, as well. It won't be long before the hinges come off again.'

'You need a way of taking the force out of the swing, Malcolm. A spring, perhaps? Maybe Andrew could come up with something. He's a woodworker, isn't he? You should ask him to look at it.'

'You're right. I'll ask him. We can't go on like this all summer.'

'Where is he this morning, anyway?'

'Up there somewhere,' Malcolm said, nodding over his shoulder.

'In the mountains? Lucky him!'

'Coire Lagan, I think he said. He was going up there again to get some rocks for Fiona's geology lesson.'

'Geology lesson?' Gwen laughed with disbelief. 'At her age?'

'It's part of her schooling, Andrew said.' Malcolm grinned and added, 'I never had schooling like that girl has.'

'Me neither. That's amazing.'

'So is little Fiona. She's a very clever girl.'

'You're right there. She is. That it? Finished?'

'Yeah.' Malcolm stood up and dusted the knees of his jeans. Then he tested the gate.

'It'll do for now,' he said. 'But I'll ask Andrew to have a look at it when he gets back. See if he can come up with a permanent solution.'

Gwen had moved on in her mind. 'Coire Lagan, eh? How long will it take him to get up and down?'

'I'm not really sure. Three or four hours, probably.'

'How I envy him! I would love to go up there, and see what it's like. Very peaceful and beautiful, I should think. You'll have seen it, too, have you, Malcolm?'

He shook his head. 'Not me. At least, not since I was just a young boy. Father took us up there one time, I seem to remember. But that was a long time ago.'

'No interest in going back now?'

Again he shook his head. 'I've got better things to do — and too much work anyway.'

'Pity. You could have taken me.'

'You fancy that, do you?'

She shook her head and sighed. 'One day, perhaps. When this old leg of mine gets a bit better, and the rest of me is a bit fitter.'

'Oh, that won't be long. Your leg's getting better every day. Even I can see that. You'll be up there with the best of them before much longer.'

'Thank you, Malcolm!' Gwen chuckled. 'You've really cheered me up. Made my day! Are you seeing Ellen tonight, by the way?'

He nodded. 'Do you want to come?'

'No, not tonight, thanks. But thank you for asking. Enjoy yourselves!'

She turned to head for the cottage, but Malcolm called her back.

'What are you doing this afternoon?' he asked. 'Anything special?'

'Not really, no. Why?'

'I was wondering if I could ask a favour of you.'

'Anything! Go on,' she said with a smile. 'What is it?'

'Ellen's birthday is coming up in a week or two, and . . . '

'Oh? What's the date? I must get her a card.'

Malcolm told her, and then continued, 'What I was wondering was if you would come with me to Broadford to help me choose a birthday present for her?'

'You're struggling to think of something, I assume? And you don't want to go to Portree, where there are more shops, in case you bump into her? Is that it?'

Malcolm laughed and looked a bit sheepish. 'Not exactly, no. What it is, there's a very nice knitwear shop in Broadford — a craft shop — that has all sorts of knitted clothes. I thought I would get her a sweater from there. The trouble is, I'm colour-blind. So I wanted your advice on colour.

'Also,' he added, looking even more sheepish, 'I wanted your advice on size. You're about the same . . . well, the same . . . '

'Shape? Size?' Gwen interjected with a smile. 'Is that what you're thinking?'

'Exactly,' he admitted, looking relieved.

She thought about it a moment, trying to visualise Ellen.

'I don't think we are the same size, Malcolm. Ellen's stronger built than me, and a bit bigger, but I suppose we're not too different. I can probably make a good guess. Yes, I'd be happy to come with you. What time would you like to go?'

# 23

A few days later, Gwen arranged to meet Ellen in Portree for lunch. It was a working day for Ellen, so they wouldn't have a lot of time. But Gwen needed to do some shopping at the supermarket, and it was too good an opportunity to miss meeting, if only for a sandwich and a bowl of soup.

'What?' Ellen demanded as they took seats in a little café they both liked. 'Why are you looking at me like that? Have I got porridge on my face from breakfast?'

Gwen laughed and shook her head. 'Of course not! I was just wondering what size you are. I saw a lovely dress in a shop, but it would be too small for me, unfortunately.'

That wasn't the truth, of course. She had had to lie desperately to cover up what she was really wondering: had she got the size right when she and Malcolm had been gift-hunting?

'If it's too small for you,' Ellen said, 'there's no hope at all of it fitting me.'

Gwen knew that to be true.

'Besides,' Ellen added sadly, 'what would I do with a new dress? We never go anywhere where I could wear it. What was it like?'

More invention was required, then. Gwen began to feel a bit desperate. She needed to change the subject before Ellen asked which shop the dress was in, so she could see it for herself.

'Changing the subject, Ellen, I've been visited a lot lately by little Fiona. She comes most days now.'

'Do you feed her? Sweets, chocolate, pop? That could be why.'

'Ellen!' Gwen laughed happily. 'Fiona is a little girl, not a bird or a mouse! Mind you, we usually do have something together. She's charming company. But I don't know quite why I've been singled out for such frequent visiting.'

'She must have taken a shine to you.

What do you talk about?'

Gwen shrugged. 'Not a lot. She's a pretty quiet, solemn little thing. A lot of the time we're both sketching — in silence. I get on with my work stuff, and Fiona draws happy families.'

'There you are, then. She likes drawing, and you give her a comfortable space to do it. Andrew does his best, but . . . '

She broke off to attend to her sandwich, which was falling to bits, scraps of tomato and lettuce cascading on all sides.

'You're such a messy eater, Ellen,' Gwen observed, laughing. 'I need to keep well clear of you.'

Ellen growled and grimaced at her. 'I should have had something safe, like your panini. Anyway, Fiona. Is she artistic? I mean, does she show any talent for sketching?'

'She does, actually. She puts a lot of feeling into those drawings. They're primitive in a sense, like cartoons, but it's easy to see what she means.'

'And what does she mean?'

Gwen sighed and pushed her plate away. 'To me, she seems to be drawing the family she would like to be part of, the family she hasn't had but still misses.'

'Makes sense. Not too surprising, when you think about it.'

'No, it isn't.'

'So she's artistic, like her father.'

'Andrew? I thought you said he was a craftsman — that he makes staircases?'

'He does now, or he did until he had to start looking after Fiona full-time. But before that, he was always artistic. He went to art school at the university in Dundee, you know.'

'Oh?'

'But he didn't like drawing for comics, which was what most of the kids there were going to do. So he quit.'

'Comics?' Gwen laughed. 'I don't understand. What are you talking about?'

'Dundee, where DC Thomson are located. The publisher? They've always done most of the comics — *The Beano, The Dandy*, and all those.

'In the olden days, it used to be said that if you grew up in Dundee, you went to work in jute, jam, or comics. They were the main traditional industries. I don't suppose it's like that now, though. The jute industry will have disappeared long ago. Probably after India became independent. But they still make jam there, I suppose, and the comics still get published. Perhaps it hasn't changed as much as you might think.'

Gwen shook her head. 'Honestly, Ellen! You're a walking encyclopaedia. How do you know all that stuff?'

'Beats me,' Ellen said, shaking her head. 'From working in a bank, probably,' she added, breaking into raucous laughter.

'Anyway,' Gwen said, when they had both calmed down a bit, 'what did Andrew do next? Did he move on from Dundee?'

'Yes, he did. He studied fine art at

some other university. Edinburgh? I'm not sure. But after a while, he decided he didn't like that any better. So he left there as well.'

'What was the problem there?'

'I don't know, really. You'll have to ask him. What Malcolm told me is that he decided he preferred working with his hands to doing academic art. He'd always liked woodworking, and so on. As a boy, he used to make all sorts of things. So he set off down that road.'

'And found a niche making staircases?' Gwen said wonderingly. 'How intriguing.'

'That's all out the window now, of course. His love life turned out to be even more chaotic than his academic and professional life. Now his life just revolves around Fiona.'

'That's not a bad thing, is it?'

'No, of course not. She's his daughter, and he's committed to looking after her. It just seems a bit of a waste that everything else has stopped for him.'

Gwen nodded. 'I know what you

mean. Where did he used to work?'

'He was freelance. All over Scotland. Wherever the work took him, basically. He always had a base, a workshop, here in Portree, but he had to go where people wanted a fancy — and expensive! — staircase.'

Ellen glanced at her watch. 'Goodness! That time already. I must fly.'

'Before you go, Ellen — something I was wondering about. You said Fiona had been ill. Did she have a problem with her legs? Did she hurt them, or something?'

Ellen frowned. 'Now you mention it, there was something like that, something I must have overheard. I don't know what, though. Why do you ask?'

'Oh, just one or two things Fiona has said that made me wonder.'

'You'll have to ask Malcolm. He'll know.'

'Yes. I will.'

Ellen pushed her chair back and got to her feet. 'OK for a walk on Saturday?'

'Yes, of course,' Gwen said, smiling. 'I'm looking forward to it. Bye, Ellen!'

Afterwards, on her own, she found herself ruminating over the things Ellen had said. She wondered what had happened with Fiona. She appeared to be perfectly all right now, but it seemed that she had had something wrong with her for a time, and perhaps had still.

Then there was Andrew, and the strange, uneven life he seemed to have led. It all made her own life seem so straightforward, boringly so. She didn't think she would have wanted to swap with him, though.

# 24

'What have you got there, Fiona?'

'It's wool from a sheep. I found it.'

'Did you? I hope the sheep didn't lose it.'

Fiona shook her head. 'It's spare wool. They don't need so much now it's getting warmer.'

'Oh? I see. Well, come on inside. It's not terribly warm out there this afternoon, is it? I just hope the sheep doesn't regret losing some of its wool.'

'The sheep don't mind the cold too much. They're tough, like me.'

Gwen hid a smile. 'That's good to know.'

The little girl stepped inside and took off her hat and coat without it being suggested. Gwen smiled openly at her. It was lovely how much she seemed to feel at home in the cottage.

'What's that nice smell? Have you

been baking a cake?'

'A few scones, actually. Would you like one?'

Fiona thought she would. She settled at the big table. Gwen made a cup of tea for herself and poured a glass of lemonade for her visitor. Then she buttered a couple of scones. How domestic we are! she thought with amusement.

'What did you do this morning, Fiona?'

'Some sums with Daddy. Then some writing. But I like drawing best. I thought I would draw this sheep's wool now — afterwards, I mean. After the scones.'

'Yes. That would be best.'

'I could do it while you're working?' Fiona suggested.

'All right. There is something I need to do.'

There wasn't really. She had done enough for one day. But she was happy to spend a quiet half-hour or so sketching while Fiona practised her drawing skills. It would be interesting to see what she made of the sheep's wool, though. That wouldn't be an easy subject.

Gwen wondered if the idea had come to Fiona because she knew she herself was interested in natural materials. She wouldn't be surprised. Fiona was bright as a button. Nothing went on without her noticing, and trying it out for herself if that was possible.

'Would you like to go to Coire Lagan?' Fiona asked suddenly.

'Coire Lagan?' Gwen repeated, surprised. Where has that come from, she wondered?

'It's in the mountains.'

'Yes, I know where it is. And, yes, I would like to go there. Have you been?'

Fiona shook her head. 'Not yet. But I know you want to go, because Uncle Malcolm said so. I do, too. It's very high up.'

'Indeed it is. But one day we'll both get there, I'm sure.'

Fiona didn't add anything further.

She began to scribble furiously. Little Big Ears! Gwen thought affectionately. You've overheard somebody's conversation again, haven't you? She shook her head, amused. Can't keep anything a secret with you around!

'You would make a very good private investigator, Fiona.'

'What's one of them?'

'Somebody who hears and sees things, and solves mysteries, such as missing people.'

'Yes,' the little girl agreed, looking up with a thoughtful expression. 'I would be good at that.'

Heavy knocking on the front door interrupted their sketching session.

'Goodness!' Gwen exclaimed. 'Who can that be?'

It sounded urgent. She got up and hurried to the door.

'Hello, Andrew!'

'Is Fiona here?' he demanded without preamble.

'Why, yes! She is. Come on in.'

'Get her, please.'

Taken aback by his gruff manner, she said, 'Of course. Is something wrong?'

'Just get her.'

With eyebrows raised, Gwen turned and called, 'Fiona! Your daddy's here.'

Fiona appeared. Andrew took her firmly by the hand.

'I'm doing some drawing,' Fiona said.

'You're going home now,' Andrew said frostily.

'Is something wrong, Andrew?' Gwen asked anxiously. 'Has something happened?'

He turned to her and said, 'What do you think you're playing at? You had no right to keep my daughter here. I had no idea where she was. I was worried to death about her.'

Gwen's hand flew up to her mouth. 'Oh, Andrew! I'm so sorry. I thought you knew.'

'How could I know? If Jeannie in the shop hadn't spotted her coming this way, I would still be searching for her. I thought she must have collapsed somewhere.'

His anger was plain to see in his face. Gwen shrugged helplessly. 'I'm so sorry. I assumed . . . '

Without waiting for her to complete her sentence, Andrew wheeled round and set off, pulling Fiona after him. The little girl gave Gwen a last, lingering glance, and then struggled to keep up with him.

Oh, dear! Gwen thought despairingly. What have I done?

# 25

Gwen was mortified. How terrible! How could she have allowed Fiona to visit without letting her father — or someone! — know where she was? Poor Andrew. He must have been worried sick.

She thought back to the beginning of Fiona's visits. Surely she had asked her, and Fiona had said her father knew where she was? She was sure she had asked her. After that, she had just taken it for granted that Andrew knew, and perhaps even approved.

But she should have continued to check each time. She could see that now. It was just that Glenbrittle was such a safe environment she hadn't bothered — hadn't even thought of it, in fact. And Fiona seemed to wander around freely all day, every day, anyway.

Yet there was a difference between

wandering around in full view and disappearing from sight. She could see that.

So, however you explained it, she was in the wrong. Poor Andrew, she thought again. He had been so angry, he hadn't been interested in hearing an apology or explanation. Not at all. Well, perhaps that was understandable. And she couldn't see that she could do anything about it now. She was simply in the wrong. And that was that.

She hesitated, thinking. There were other things troubling her about the scene that had just been played out at her front door. Why on earth had Andrew thought Fiona had collapsed? That seemed a strange thing to say.

And he had been so hostile. Extraordinarily hostile. She couldn't think of another word to describe it. Had that really been justified? She couldn't believe her negligence, or stupidity — call it what you like — had really justified all that anger and contempt.

Horrible man! she decided finally

with a sigh. People were right about him.

The incident had upset her profoundly. There was no doubt about that. She didn't get much sleep that night, her mind rehearsing the things she might have done and said to avert it happening. To no avail, of course. What was done was done. She couldn't make it any better. She just had to get on with things. Move on, and try to recover.

Much as she lectured herself sensibly, though, it seemed to make no difference. She still felt utterly miserable. The entire summer seemed to have been tarnished. She couldn't shake the mood in the next few days, either. After a while, she even wondered if she wanted to stay in Glenbrittle. The dreadful scene with Andrew had taken away all her joy and delight about being there.

Even more disappointingly, Ellen seemed cold and indifferent when she told her what had happened at their next lunch meeting.

'You must do what you think best,'

Ellen said with a shrug. 'Do whatever you want.'

Gwen found that response hurtful. It wasn't what she had wanted, or expected, to hear from a woman she had come to regard as her friend. Leave or stay. Ellen didn't much care either way, it seemed.

'Is that the best advice you can give me, Ellen? It's not like you.'

'Gwen . . . ' Ellen stopped herself and said, 'What do you want from me, Gwen?'

It was a good question. What did she want?

'Nothing, really, I suppose,' she said sadly. 'I just thought . . . I hoped you might be more forgiving. That's all. I know it was stupid of me not to make sure Andrew knew where Fiona was, I admit it. But was Andrew's rage entirely justified?'

Ellen shrugged again and looked away. 'I have no idea.'

Gwen stirred her coffee. 'I thought I was doing something good,' she said sadly. 'I was being a friend to Fiona, and occupying her for part of the day when Andrew and everyone else was busy. Besides, I like Fiona. I . . . '

'Look, Gwen, I warned you what Andrew was like. Didn't I warn you — more than once?'

Gwen sighed and nodded.

'He has always had problems with other people. Relationship problems. Arrogance, impatience, superiority, quick temper — call it what you like! But the result is the same. Andrew is a very difficult man. That's why I advised you to keep well clear of him. You should have listened.'

'Perhaps he would hear another apology from me now he's calmed down?'

Ellen shook her head. 'Forget it! Another characteristic is that he is relentlessly unforgiving.'

'No hope at all of getting things back on an even keel?'

'None.' Ellen glanced at her watch and added, 'I must fly.'

'If you must.'

'What does that mean?'

Gwen shrugged. 'Nothing.'

'And another thing,' Ellen snapped, seemingly stung by something Gwen had said or done, or not said or done, 'I'm not happy about you seeing Malcolm on the side.'

'What?'

'Think about it.'

'I have no idea what you mean, Ellen.'

'Oh, I think you do. I'm not happy about you having lunch with Malcolm, and keeping it secret from me.'

While Gwen was still trying to sort out what that meant, Ellen pushed her chair back and got up to go.

'Ellen, I think . . . '

'Think what you like — and do what you like! I don't care.'

Aghast, Gwen watched open-mouthed as her erstwhile friend marched out of the café.

She hadn't even left any money to cover her share of the bill, Gwen thought belatedly and inconsequentially.

Later, much later, back at the cottage, she thought long and hard about whether she should stay in Glenbrittle. She felt so miserable, and there seemed to be no way out of the hole she had not so much dug for herself as found herself in. Perhaps it really was time to go. Home beckoned. She even thought nostalgically of Rob, which she hadn't done before.

Tomorrow, she thought. I'll let it rest overnight and see how I feel in the morning. If nothing has changed, I'll go. There's no point staying somewhere I'm not happy.

# 26

The next day, she felt no different. Things had changed. People seemed to have changed. This was no longer a friendly, welcoming place for her. She was out of her depth. It was time she was gone.

After all, she had a life back in Yorkshire. She had a wonderful job there, and she could live with her parents for a while until she got sorted out with somewhere of her own again. And there was Rob.

What was so bad about Rob that she had dumped him? She had long forgiven him for the injuries she had suffered in the car crash. It had been a tenible accident, at least partly brought about by his habitual drunkenness, but things like that happened all the time, often with far worse consequences.

They hadn't gone to the party

intending to get plastered. They were both old enough to be past that stage in their lives. It had just happened. If they had decided beforehand that one of them would be the driver, and the other the passenger, they would have been all right. She could have driven, as she so often did, while Rob gently got sozzled. Or vice-versa. It had happened before, plenty of times. Now she couldn't think why it hadn't happened then, too.

When you thought about it like that, of course, the accident had been as much her fault as Rob's. She should have been more aware, and more organised. But she'd got lazy, or tired perhaps. For once, she hadn't managed to manage Rob and his propensity to drink too much. Once had been enough.

Otherwise? If it wasn't the accident, what else could be laid at Rob's door to justify her decision to split with him? Not a lot, when you thought about it. He was a good, decent man. Popular socially. Hardworking. Attentive to her.

They could have had a good life together. They still could, she decided, pushing aside the breakfast pots. Rob wouldn't have changed. Time to do something about it.

She started collecting her things together. The cases and bags came out. Things went into them. Packing the car began. She needed to contact Mrs McIver, and one or two other people perhaps, and she wanted to take a last little walk along the seashore, but she also felt a need to put her decision into action. She didn't think she would be able to do all that and then actually get away today, but a departure tomorrow would be possible. That would be soon enough, anyway.

★　★　★

On her walk later that morning, as she headed back towards the cottage, she bumped into Malcolm, who was carrying a fishing rod and four little fish he had caught. She was glad to see him.

He was someone who hadn't turned against her — not yet, at least.

'What have you got there, Malcolm?'

'Herrings,' he said proudly, holding the fish out for her to inspect. 'It's the start of the season. At least, a few of them are starting to arrive.'

'Lovely,' she said, examining and admiring his catch. 'Well done! I didn't know you were a fisherman, Malcolm.'

'Occasional one only. But herring are pretty easy to catch.'

'You're being far too modest! It won't have been all that easy, I'm sure.'

Malcolm grinned. 'What are you up to this fine day?'

She took a deep breath. It was time to stop dissimulating, time to lay it out for someone. It might as well be Malcolm.

'I'm glad I bumped into you, Malcolm. I wouldn't want to have gone without saying goodbye to you. I'm leaving, probably tomorrow.'

'Leaving?' he repeated, astounded. 'What's happened? Emergency at home?'

She shook her head. 'No, nothing like

that. It's just that things are not working out here for me, after all.'

'What things? I thought everything was fine?'

'Well, my work for one. That's not going too well. Then I seem to have fallen out with everyone — apart from you, of course,' she hastened to add.

'Who? Who have you fallen out with?'

'Andrew, for one. Ellen, for another.'

Malcolm looked stunned. 'What's happened with you and Ellen? I thought you were great friends?'

'So did I. You'll have to ask her,' she added with a shrug.

'I will. Andrew is looking for you, by the way. He was going to go over to the cottage this morning. He's probably there now.'

She grimaced. What to do now? She definitely did not want to meet Andrew again. On the other hand, she was not going to avoid him deliberately either. That would be taking things too far.

'I'll see him, if he's there,' she said

reluctantly, turning away.

Oh, why did everything have to be so complicated, and people so difficult?

# 27

They met halfway between the camp-site and the cottage. Neutral ground, she thought. Good.

'Good morning, Gwen!'

'Andrew.'

'I was hoping I'd see you.'

'Oh?'

He didn't look so fierce and angry as he had the last time she had seen him. That was just as well. She had decided she would give as good as she got. If he was in the same mood, they could have a public slanging match.

'I want to apologise, Gwen. What I said to you the other day was completely over the top. And unforgivable. I'm sorry.'

She was taken aback. It took a moment or two for her to rearrange her thoughts and lower her high alert.

'That's OK, Andrew. Don't worry

about it. You were upset.'

'I was upset,' he admitted. 'But that's no excuse.'

'Anyway,' Gwen added, 'I was in the wrong myself. I should have made sure you knew where Fiona was. I'd just become so used to her visits that I didn't even think about it when she came the other day.'

'Visits? More than one?'

Gwen nodded. 'She's been coming to see me practically every day for a while now.'

'I see. I didn't know that.'

Andrew turned and gazed out to sea, as if expecting something unusual to happen out there. She sensed that he, too, was having to process something new, and finding it difficult.

He turned back to her. 'What do you do with her when she visits?'

'Mostly we've been drawing — sketching. I have my work, and she has things she likes to draw.'

He nodded, understanding now. 'She likes to draw,' he admitted.

'Takes after her father, I assume?' Gwen said with a reluctant smile.

He just nodded. He seemed to be at a loss as to what to say to her. She felt a little sorry for him. If she hadn't been so blown away by his rage the other day, she might have felt even more sorry for him. An apology now was fine, but it didn't wash everything away.

The people she had spoken to about him had all been right, basically. Personal relationships, and even simple interactions with other people, really were difficult for him. Not that that excused him, in her view. He had been insufferably rude to her, and had brought her plans for the summer crashing down.

'Malcolm spoke to me,' he said now, quietly.

'Oh? Is that so unusual?'

He shook his head. 'About you. He said you would like to go up to Coire Lagan.'

'Really? He said that?' She wondered how on earth that conversation had developed.

'He said you're not confident enough to do it on your own yet,' he explained, with a glance towards her leg.

What was that to do with him — with either of the brothers? Gwen was beginning to find the conversation irritating. Where on earth was it leading?

'We could go together,' Andrew added suddenly. 'You'd be fine along with me.'

Goodness! she thought. Is that an invitation? It rather sounds as if it is.

'That's very kind of you, Andrew, but I'm afraid it won't be possible now. You see, I'll be leaving tomorrow. I've decided.'

'Leaving?' He looked astonished. 'I didn't know that.'

'Well, it's only just been decided. I haven't got round to telling everyone yet. In fact, the first thing I'm going to do when I get back to the cottage is phone your mother.'

Andrew studied his boots for a moment and then looked directly at her. 'I'm sorry,' he said. 'Any particular reason?'

'No, no!' she lied. 'Just one thing on top of another. A big consideration is that my work isn't going as well as I'd hoped it would. It's time I got back to my roots, I think.'

Andrew nodded, but he didn't seem happy. There were things on his mind that she couldn't even guess were there. She had no idea how this man's mind worked. An enigma? At least!

'How is Fiona?' she asked to divert him.

'Fiona?' He hesitated. 'She'd been much better for a while, but she's not so good again at the moment.'

'Oh? What's wrong with her?'

He pushed his hands deep into his trouser pockets and kicked out at a stone on the path before he replied.

'Fiona has problems. She's had them for a while.'

'With her legs?'

He glanced quickly at her and nodded. 'Her legs, yes. They don't always work properly.'

Gwen was shocked, as much as anything because her guess, based on things Fiona had said and she herself had deduced, seemed to have been accurate.

'What's wrong with her legs?'

He blew out heavily and kicked at another stone. 'They don't seem to know, the doctors. Not really. The problem comes and goes. We have to manage it, that's all. When it's bad she just stays in bed. It's a large part of why she gets home tuition instead of going to school.'

'Is that why you were so concerned the other day that she might have collapsed?'

He nodded. 'She was all right, though, as it happened. Thankfully. Well, I must get on,' he said straightening up.

'Please give Fiona my love,' Gwen said. 'I hope she feels better soon.'

'I will. Well, good luck,' he said finally.

Then he turned away and set off back to sort out his other problems. There seemed to be quite a few of them. She watched him go for a moment, and then turned to resume her walk back to the cottage.

# 28

Back at the cottage, she phoned Mrs McIver. Explaining and apologising to her for the change of plan had to be top of her agenda. There were financial considerations for the McIvers, as well as the sheer courtesy factor. Other potential visitors to the cottage would have been turned away because it had been let for the season. So Gwen was fully prepared to continue paying, perhaps until the cottage could be re-let. She was sure they could reach an amicable agreement.

Not yet, they couldn't. Mrs McIver wasn't answering the phone. All Gwen got was a voice asking her to leave a message. She sighed and put the phone down.

What next? More packing, she decided. There was plenty more of that to do. First, though, she would have a cup of coffee. She deserved it after her walk, and after meeting Andrew.

What a strange man he was. Hard as iron — and just as communicative! Yet, beneath that, there seemed to be a decent human being struggling to emerge. He had done his best to make amends, which he hadn't really needed to.

His apology had been surprising, but also very welcome. It made his disproportionate response the other day seem more understandable, and more acceptable, especially when it was coupled with his concern about Fiona's health. Gwen felt that she herself had certainly been in the wrong, but so too had been Andrew. At least he seemed to know that now, which made her feel a bit better.

Fiona had not been much in her thoughts the past couple of days, but she thought about her now. It was such a pity how things had ended, with the little girl dragged away home, and now not very well either. Before she left in the morning, she would try to find her to say goodbye. That was the least she could do.

Perhaps she could leave her some drawing materials, too. She would have liked to do more for her, but what else could she do? She shrugged. Nothing, really. Anyway, she was just another summer visitor to Glenbrittle. Soon there would be plenty of others to take her place.

Just after twelve-thirty, she heard someone knock on the front door. Whoever could that be? she wondered as she struggled to bring a heavy bag downstairs. She dropped the bag. Better go and see.

A visibly distraught Andrew confronted her when she opened the door.

'What is it?' she asked, alarmed.

'Is Fiona here?'

'No, of course not. I haven't seen her since . . . '

'Nor has anyone else. She's missing.'

'Missing?'

Fiona roamed around so much it was

hard to know how she could be missing, or even how anyone would notice if she was.

'We have a maths lesson scheduled, and she isn't here for it. She likes maths,' Andrew added.

Gwen didn't know what to say. 'Perhaps she's just visiting someone else?'

Andrew shook his head. 'We've been all around the campsite, Malcolm and me. Jeannie as well.'

Gwen knew that was the woman who worked in the shop.

'We can't find her,' Andrew added, twisting and turning, as if he hoped to see Fiona appear at any moment.

'She's not here, Andrew,' Gwen said gently. 'What about the beach?'

He shook his head. 'She's not there.'

He spun round, eyes searching. Gwen wondered if he was justified in being so agitated. Then their earlier conversation came to mind, and she understood his distress. Something might have happened to her.

'We have a rule,' Andrew said now. 'She says where she's going, and she always appears for her lessons. She wouldn't miss one. She never has. I must look for her.'

He turned and began walking away.

'Wait, Andrew!' Gwen called. 'I'll come with you.'

\* \* \*

They searched all around the campsite, as did others who had been notified by Malcolm and Andrew. None of the campers had seen Fiona that morning. Some joined in the search, volunteering to look further afield along the coast, in case she had wandered off in that direction. Gwen went inland with Andrew, heading towards the nearby farm.

'Does she often come this way?' Gwen asked.

He shook his head. 'Not to my knowledge. She doesn't like the cows.'

'Too big for her?' Gwen asked lightly.

'Something like that.'

Not surprisingly, he was even more terse than usual. Outwardly, he wasn't panicking. There wasn't much to see. But she could feel the nervous energy radiating from him. He was shaking with it.

'Where does she like to play?' she asked, trying to distract him and release some of all that bottled-up anxiety. 'The beach, of course. Does she go in the sea?'

'Occasionally, but never by herself.'

'Perhaps she has a secret den somewhere?'

He just nodded. Clearly, if she did, her father was unaware of it. But then, if he had been, it wouldn't be secret, would it?

There was no sign of her around the farm, and the people who ran the farm said they hadn't seen a little girl that morning. They readily took them on a guided tour of their property in case Fiona had stowed herself away somewhere. Nothing. They found nothing to suggest the girl had been anywhere near, either.

On the way back to the campsite, Gwen felt Andrew was about to burst — either literally, or into a run. She laid a restraining hand on his arm.

'If you want to go on ahead, Andrew, then do. I shan't mind. But perhaps we could just talk for a minute or two first? Can we put our heads together, and think about where she might have gone?'

She put it that way because it was better to think that wherever Fiona was, she had gone there herself. The alternative — that she had been taken, possibly against her will — was too distressing to contemplate.

'When did you last see her, Andrew?'

'At breakfast this morning. Eight o'clock.'

'That was when the meal was over?'

He nodded. 'She went off out then. I was pleased. I thought her wanting to go out was a good sign.'

'In what way?'

'I hoped it meant the problem with her legs must have eased.'

Gwen thought about that. Perhaps it was a good sign.

'What happens when her leg problem starts up again? I mean, is she in pain?'

Andrew looked bleakly at her. 'Pain, yes. And she can't stand up, literally.'

'Then you're right. It was a good sign.' She thought some more. 'Was there anything at all unusual about her this morning?'

'Nothing,' he said, considering. 'Not that I noticed.'

'What was she wearing? Just a summer dress?'

'Oh, no! She was wearing plenty. She had her jacket on, the one with the hood.'

'On a beautiful summer morning?'

He shrugged. 'She knows how soon it can change here, and be cold and wet. I've told her often enough.'

'So, nothing out of the ordinary?' Gwen asked again as they walked on.

'Nothing. She wasn't upset, or

anything, if that's what you mean? I hadn't had to tell her off. And she ate plenty. More than usual, in fact.'

'What did she have?'

'Cereal and a boiled egg. She even had a cup of tea. So she wasn't off her food.'

'Tea? Does she drink tea?'

'Not usually, no.'

'Why today?'

'I have no idea. She just said she would like some.'

They walked on in silence for a couple of minutes, Andrew worrying, Gwen thinking.

'So the tea was unusual,' she said thoughtfully.

'What of it?' he snapped. 'She had a big pile of toast, as well!'

'A lot?'

'Half-a-dozen slices, probably. I don't know. I was in and out of the kitchen myself, and Fiona can use the toaster.'

That was the clincher, so far as Gwen was concerned. She took a deep breath.

'Andrew, I think Fiona had planned

to go out for the day. She was stocking up on nutrition, and probably planning to take food with her.'

He stopped and spun round to stare at her. 'I never thought of that,' he said wonderingly. 'I wonder if you're right.'

'She must have planned it.'

'But where could she have gone?'

'I think I might know,' Gwen said, as calmly as she could manage as her pulse rate shot skywards.

'You know?' he asked, incredulous.

She nodded. 'It's just a guess, really, but I'm pretty sure of it.'

And she was, too.

# 29

He stared at her, waiting to be convinced.

'What have you got in mind?'

Gwen hesitated. Was she right? She didn't really know — how could she? — but she felt instinctively that the answer that had come to her in a flash was right.

'Andrew, I think she's gone to Coire Lagan.'

'Coire Lagan?'

She nodded.

He said nothing for a moment. Then he said, 'How do you work that out?'

Mercifully, he hadn't rejected the idea with contempt — not yet, anyway! She took a deep breath.

'Fiona and I have talked about it once or twice. She said she hasn't been but would like to, and she knows how much I would like to go there. We talked about it,' she added with a shrug, her justification fizzling out in the face of Andrew's blank stare. Although he didn't say anything, it was obvious what he thought: she was an idiot!

'Is that all you have?' he asked.

She nodded. 'I know it isn't much, but my instincts tell me it's where she will have gone. I think we should go there. We've looked everywhere else.'

'Instincts?' he said slowly.

She braced herself for a contemptuous dismissal, and steeled herself to come out fighting.

'I believe in instinct,' he said suddenly. 'It's how the things that really matter get done. Let's go!'

Andrew didn't ask her if she was up for it. He just seemed to assume she was going with him when he struck off across the fields, heading for the slopes where the foot of the heather-clad mountains met the floor of the glen. Nor did Gwen herself question what she was going to do. She simply went with him. Coire Lagan was where they

201

were both going.

This was Andrew's home ground, and he could probably have found the route even blindfolded. He led the way across the fields until they hit a muddy footpath that took them up the lower slopes. On the flat, Gwen managed to keep up with him, but when the ground became steeper she struggled and began to fall behind. Andrew glanced over his shoulder and paused when he realised what was happening.

'You go on!' she gasped. 'Don't wait for me.'

'It's all right. Catch your breath.'

'How long to the lochan?' she managed to get out after a few moments.

'An hour. Maybe a bit longer.'

That didn't sound too bad. But if she was wrong, they were going to lose a couple of hours of valuable time. Was she wrong? Already she was having doubts, and wondering if a six-year old could get up here on her own.

It wasn't worth thinking about, she decided. They had to go on, and find out for themselves.

'There's some bad weather coming in,' Andrew remarked, sounding anxious. 'It's a good thing she has her proper jacket with her.'

Gwen turned and looked out across the bay. Once again she saw low-lying cloud pulsing towards them.

'We'd better get on,' Andrew added.

She knew he meant before visibility became poor. It wasn't the possibility of rain that worried him.

'Lead on!' she urged, giving him a smile to encourage him.

He nodded and turned to start climbing again.

★   ★   ★

The cloud swept across the lower slopes and enveloped them in minutes. Gwen felt its moist, cool grip, and shivered, almost despairing. If Fiona was up here, how could they ever find her in this? The poor little thing would be lost and scared, and soon wet and cold.

Oh, she hoped she wasn't here! She hoped she was just plain wrong, even if that meant having to face up to Andrew's contempt, which would surely be forthcoming.

She caught up with him suddenly. His broad back appeared in front of her through the mist. 'Not far now,' he said, turning towards her. 'How are you doing?'

'Better than I expected,' she responded breathlessly. Her hand swept up to her pounding heart. 'Keep going!'

Andrew nodded and resumed his steady uphill trod. She worked hard to keep the gap between them to a minimum.

'Do you still know where we are, Andrew?' she called.

'Aye. I know this path fine well.'

But Fiona won't, Gwen thought, wincing. She hasn't been up here before. Not ever. If she's here now, that is, which is a pretty big if.

'You were right,' Andrew cried suddenly. 'She is up here!'

# 30

'What have you seen?' Gwen demanded.

Andrew pointed at the ground. 'Her footprint!'

There, in soft mud, was a small footprint, a child's footprint.

'It's not necessarily Fiona's,' Gwen pointed out, worried he was jumping to conclusions.

'It is.' Andrew nodded with conviction. 'She's wearing her wellies. I recognise the print. Come on!'

Gwen had her doubts. How likely was it that Fiona's rubber boots were unique? Not very, in her opinion.

On the other hand, she had to admit with reluctant but growing excitement, that print was very recent. How many other children with feet that size could have been up here this morning?

The cloud stayed with them, and the rain it had brought persisted. It was cold now, too, rather than just cool. The heat generated by their exertions suggested otherwise, but Gwen knew the air was cold. She hoped Fiona really was well clothed.

Andrew began casting about, head weaving like a foxhound's. His pace slowed.

'What's wrong?' she asked.

'I think we might have come too far.'

'But we're not there yet, are we?'

'No, but . . . ' He came to a stop so sharply that she cannoned into him. 'Hear that?'

She shook her head. 'Why do you think we've come too far?'

'I haven't seen any more footprints. We should have, on this wet ground we've been crossing.'

Gwen hadn't thought of that. She hadn't been looking, either. All her focus had been on putting one foot in front of the other, in her attempt to keep up with Andrew.

'There it is again!' he exclaimed, looking at her.

This time she had heard it, a child's cry for help. 'It's Fiona,' she said without hesitation now, her heart beating faster than ever.

Andrew plunged back down the track, calling to his daughter as he ran. Gwen followed as best she could.

They found her a little way off the track, huddled in the heather. She was cold and wet, and shivering, but seemingly in good spirits.

'I knew you would come,' she said as Andrew collected her in his arms. 'I just knew you would!'

'Did you now?' Andrew said, his eyes closed with relief as he hugged her.

Gwen watched on, smiling, every bit as relieved as he was.

'I heard you — so I shouted!' Fiona gushed.

'And I heard you,' Andrew said, struggling to control his emotions.

Gwen closed her eyes for a moment in a silent prayer of thanks.

Then Fiona caught sight of Gwen. Her eyes widened with surprise and she shrieked a greeting.

'Gwen!'

'Hello, Fiona! How are you? Have you hurt yourself?'

'My foot hurts,' Fiona confessed.

'Not your leg?'

'No. My foot.'

Andrew immediately sat down with her, tugged off her boot and gently moved her foot in different directions. 'It's your ankle, isn't it?' he said after a few moments of study.

'Yes,' Fiona said uncertainly. 'My ankle on my foot.'

Gwen hid a smile. She was so relieved and happy to see Fiona that she scarcely knew what to say. One hurting foot didn't seem to matter. Fortunately, Andrew was equal to the occasion.

'It's these boots,' he said now. 'You shouldn't have come up here in your wellies, Fiona. I've told you that before. In fact, you shouldn't have come up here at all on your own. I've told you that, as well.'

'I wanted to,' Fiona said.

'Even so ... You should have said something. We've been looking all over for you.'

'Has even Gwen been looking for me?'

'Even me,' Gwen said, smiling. 'We didn't know where you were.'

'No,' Fiona said, sounding satisfied. 'You didn't.'

'But Gwen guessed,' Andrew said. 'And she was right.'

Fiona flashed Gwen a big smile. 'Gwen's my friend,' she said simply.

'Of course I am,' Gwen assured her. 'That's how I could guess where you'd gone. I know you, you little monkey!'

She turned to Andrew and asked, 'Is she very cold?'

He nodded. 'Not too bad. But we'd better get her home soon.'

Just as Gwen was wondering if Fiona could walk, Andrew pre-empted the question by hoisting her on to his shoulder and setting off downhill with her. Gwen followed as best she could.

209

Although she had been oblivious of her own condition in the desperate race uphill, her limitations were revealing themselves now. She was tired now, and various aches and pains were beginning to assert themselves, but all that was as nothing compared with her overwhelming relief that they had found Fiona safe and well. She couldn't stop smiling, however hard the rain fell.

The question of what on earth the little girl had been doing, coming up here all on her own, was one that scarcely arose. It could wait, she told herself firmly when it tried to get into her mind.

# 31

They headed back to Andrew's cottage, where Gwen helped Andrew strip Fiona of her sodden clothes and give her a hot bath to warm her up. The little girl's teeth were still chattering as they dried her with a big fluffy towel that she insisted they use, as it was her special towel, but she was in good spirits and surprisingly eager to talk.

'I knew you would come, Daddy,' she said for the umpteenth time. 'I knew you would find me.'

'You were lucky we did find you in that cloud and rain.'

'I heard you. That's why I shouted. I didn't think Gwen would come, though. I thought . . . '

'You're lucky she did!'

Gwen smiled and said, 'Shall I make you a hot drink, Fiona? Would you like that?'

'Yes, please.'

'See what you can find in the kitchen cupboard,' Andrew suggested. 'I don't know what we've got.'

There wasn't any chocolate or cocoa. So Gwen made a mug of weak tea, adding milk and plenty of sugar. By the time she had done that, Andrew had got Fiona dressed in a nightdress and wrapped in a fleece blanket.

'Here you are, Fiona. Try this.'

The little girl seized the cup and sniffed suspiciously before taking a sip. 'It's not hot chocolate,' she said, obviously disappointed.

'No, I don't think there is any.'

Andrew shook his head, confirming it. 'One of the luxuries we're without at the moment,' he said.

'Perhaps Fiona should have something to eat, as well?'

'Can you see what you can find?' he suggested.

There were plenty of eggs, Gwen discovered. So she took one and scrambled it. That seemed to go down as well as the sweet tea.

When all that was done, Andrew said to Fiona, 'One question, sweetheart, before you go to bed and have an early night. Why did you go up there today?'

Fiona shrugged but didn't otherwise respond.

'We spent a lot of time looking for you. Everybody did. The whole camp-site did, infact!'

'And Uncle Malcolm?'

'Of course.'

'What about Aunty Ellen?'

'No. She wasn't here.'

'But Gwen was, and I thought she'd gone.'

'Not yet, she hasn't. Fiona, I think we deserve to know why you went up the mountain. What were you doing?'

Fiona said nothing. She just frowned and sucked her thumb.

Andrew was about to demand an answer again, but Gwen touched his arm and gave a shake of her head when he glanced at her. 'Leave it for now, Andrew.'

After a moment's hesitation he nodded agreement.

But Fiona had noticed the exchange, and she wasn't having that. She wanted her day in court.

'I wasn't happy,' she blurted out suddenly.

'Oh?' Andrew said. 'And why was that, might I ask?'

Fiona pondered long and hard before saying defiantly, 'I wanted Gwen to be my new mummy, and you weren't very nice to her. Then Uncle Malcolm said she was leaving, and going home. So I cried. Then I went to Coire Lagan, but I don't think I got there.'

'No, you didn't,' Andrew said gently. 'But you weren't far away.'

Dear God! Gwen thought, astonished. The things that run through a child's mind and heart.

Andrew turned towards her and shook his head. Then he smiled and said softly, 'Well, now we know, don't we?'

★ ★ ★

Andrew put Fiona to bed soon afterwards. The little girl was obviously very tired after her adventurous day, and even though it was still only early evening she was happy to go. With the excitement over and the adrenaline fading, fatigue had caught up with her.

Gwen suspected she was relishing all the attention her escapade had brought her, but she couldn't find it in her heart to disapprove. Fiona led a rather lonely life here with her stern, unusual father, conscientious and dedicated to her though he obviously was. Perhaps ordinary sympathy and loving affection were in short supply. Andrew — poor man! — had his hands full, what with overcoming a failed marriage, parenting, and trying to cobble together a living.

Not that he was a man lacking in sympathy or empathy — or in emotion either, she had discovered in full today. In fact, the day's events had been a revelation in many ways. She was starting to see Andrew in a different light. Already his unfortunate outburst at her had been overtaken by a picture of a man deeply caring about his daughter, and desperate to protect her and do what was right for her. If sometimes events could threaten to overwhelm him, who could be surprised or blame him?

With Fiona safely put to bed, Andrew turned to Gwen and said quietly, 'I can't tell you how much I appreciate what you've done for us today. Here you are, on the brink of leaving to sort out your own life, and yet you dropped everything to come to our aid. And you knew intuitively where she had gone! Without you, I would never have found her. I didn't have the slightest idea where she was. You did, though, didn't you? Thank you, Gwen.'

Gwen shrugged and smiled. 'I've spent rather a lot of time with Fiona the past few weeks, and I've had many conversations with her. I suppose I've developed an idea of how her mind works, as well as getting to like her so much.'

Andrew shook his head ruefully.

'Sometimes she's a complete mystery to me, I'm afraid. I would never have thought of Coire Lagan.'

'Oh, you would! Eventually you'd have found her. My guesswork just speeded things up a bit.'

That wasn't exactly what Gwen was thinking. She knew her guess had been inspired, and quite possibly really had saved the day. It might have been next week before anyone else had thought of going where she and Andrew had gone, if they ever had.

Much more likely was that Fiona would have been stumbled across accidentally by people walking in the mountains, and by then it might well have been far too late. But that was not something to say to the girl's poor father at a time like this. Better to keep it to herself.

'As for the rest of what you said, Andrew, of course I stayed to help. I could hardly have just turned my back and returned to Yorkshire as if nothing had happened!

'I was very worried when you said Fiona was missing. All sorts of terrible things happen somewhere to young children every day. I had to help find her. Besides, it wasn't like her to just go off by herself.'

Andrew smiled at last. 'It wasn't like her. You're right. It's never happened before, either. But all's well that ends well, as they say. Thank you so much once again.

'Look, would you mind hanging on a few minutes longer, Gwen? I need to let Malcolm know everything is fine now. I did ask him to stand everyone down, but I owe him a little bit more explanation now things have settled.'

'Of course. Go ahead. I don't mind waiting. After all, we don't want Fiona waking up alone and doing another disappearing act, do we?'

Andrew gave a wry smile, shook his head, and took himself off.

# 32

What a strange man he is, she thought with a sigh and a sad smile. So full of contrasts. One minute he's as uncommunicative as a lump of stone; the next he's as caring a human being as you're likely to meet. Full of love for his daughter, too. And not just out of a sense of duty or obligation. I've seen today just how much he cares for her. He really is doing his best to be a good parent, as well as a loving one. I respect him. And, given that his daughter is little Fiona, I quite envy him.

That last thought brought to mind Fiona's explanation of why she had done what she had. She smiled and shook her head. Poor little thing! She missed her mum. At least, she knew her mum was missing. She didn't have one. What could be more natural than to be upset about that? Fiona had seemingly fixed on her as a substitute, but really, it could have been anyone who was nice to her. Gwen had just happened to be the one.

She shook her head and sighed. Then, suddenly, she found herself thinking she really was rather hungry herself. She had had very little to eat today. In the hunt for Fiona, all thoughts of food had vanished, but they were coming back now with a vengeance. She hoped Andrew wouldn't be long. She wanted to get back to the cottage and look for something to eat.

Presumably, Andrew would be much the same — hungry. Even more so, perhaps, given that he was a big, healthy man. Maybe there was something she could do about that.

She looked around the kitchen again to see if there was anything that would make a quick meal. There wasn't a lot, she soon decided. The best bet seemed to be something to do with eggs. There was a wicker basket containing a dozen or more of them. Perhaps Andrew kept chickens? Somebody must do. These were not supermarket eggs.

The back door opened behind her, as she stood there with an egg in each hand, inspecting them.

'Hungry?'

She spun round, saw Andrew, and giggled.

'Will you have something to eat with me?' he asked. 'You've certainly earned it.'

'Oh, I couldn't possibly!'

'Yes, you could.'

'Well . . . '

'Please stay, Gwen. Fiona might wake up and start looking for you,' he added with a grin.

Gwen laughed. 'If it's a serious invitation?'

'It is, yes. Mind you, I don't know what exactly I can offer. Not much, probably, at the moment. But some-thing to keep the wolf from the door. That is . . . Or perhaps you would rather just go back to your place?'

That was definitely an option worth

considering, but not for long.

'Thank you, Andrew. I would love to stay and have something with you. I was just looking around your kitchen to see what there is. Eggs, mostly, it seems.'

'Yes. We have a few chickens out the back. There's always plenty of eggs, if nothing else.'

'Well, then. How about I make us an omelette? That wouldn't take long.'

His eyes widened with interest.

'I do a good omelette,' she promised.

While Gwen made the omelette, Andrew set the table and added a loaf of bread and a dish of butter.

'I noticed a packet of salad in the fridge,' Gwen called to him. 'Shall we have that with it?'

'Good idea.'

He got that out and then went to check on Fiona while Gwen coaxed the omelette into rising.

'How is she?' Gwen asked when he returned.

'She's asleep. Well tired, I think.'

'Poor little thing!' Gwen said, chuckling. 'I should jolly well think she is tired.'

'Self-inflicted,' Andrew said with a grin as he sat down.

It sounded a harsh judgement, but Gwen didn't believe it was. Relief was still the prevailing emotion for them both. She began to carve up and dish out the omelette. Andrew watched intently.

'You must be as hungry as me,' Gwen said, laughing.

'I believe I am. Now we have her ladyship settled, hunger has come to the fore.'

'With me, too,' Gwen admitted, sitting down. 'Eat!'

There was silence for a couple of minutes. Then Andrew said, 'So you've been seeing quite a bit of my daughter while you've been here?'

Gwen shrugged. 'Yes. I suppose I have. She just appeared at the cottage one day. I don't know why. Then she started turning up on a regular basis. I was pleased she did. She's a lovely little thing and I was always glad to see her. Very good company, too. If I'm working, she doesn't interrupt. She just gets on with something herself — drawing, usually.'

'Interesting,' Andrew said as he finished off his share of the omelette. 'I worry that she spends too much time alone. So it's good to hear that she can fit in with someone else, besides me.'

'I know what you mean, but she's fine. 'Well-adjusted' is the phrase, I think.'

Gwen had long thought that it would be so much better if Fiona attended a school, and mixed with other children who she could get to know, but she wasn't going to say so uninvited. There was also Fiona's illness, or mysterious disability, to consider. Andrew had previously said that was why she had home tuition instead of going to school. So maybe the current arrangement was for the best.

'That was good,' Andrew said,

cleaning his plate of every last shred of food. 'Excellent, in fact. All day I'd forgotten to be hungry, but it had been coming back to me fast!'

'For me, too.'

Gwen smiled, thinking how remarkably normal Andrew seemed now. She had never heard him talk so much as he had these past few hours, and all of it entirely pleasant. Not a cross word. Perhaps she had misjudged him all along. Or, more likely, the day's events had just unleashed a floodtide of emotional responses to overcome his normal reticence and impatience. She hoped there would be a lasting effect, even though she wouldn't be here to witness it.

But there was one question she wanted to ask, and she felt now that she could.

'This morning, Andrew, when we first met, you said Fiona was ill again with her leg problem. So how could she have got to where we found her?'

He shook his head. 'It beats me. I have no idea. When it happens, her legs simply refuse to support her. They buckle, and she collapses in pain.

'But it comes and goes,' he added thoughtfully. 'It's not as if it's always the same.'

That sounded very odd to Gwen. She wondered aloud if Fiona really had been ill again.

'Well, she'd been fine for a while,' Andrew said. 'Then this relapse occurred a few days ago.'

'She was perfectly all right when she visited me the last time,' Gwen pointed out.

'Yes?' he said doubtfully.

'So it was after that when it came back?'

He nodded.

'And she has been all right, seemingly, ever since I arrived here. I never saw her with a problem, although she did mention that she had had trouble with her leg.'

'What are you suggesting?' Andrew asked with amusement. 'That she faked it?'

'Oh, no!' Gwen said quickly, although the possibility had actually crossed her mind. 'I was just wondering if it was — I don't know! — a psychosomatic condition, or something?'

'What does that mean?'

'As I understand the term, it means that symptoms of a physical illness are brought on by psychological factors — stress, say, or anxiety. I'm just wondering if that could be what happens with Fiona, that's all.

'The question, I suppose, is if her physical problems could be brought on by her state of mind or whatever, or if they are purely physical. It seems odd that everything should have been all right for quite some time and then she suffered a relapse.

'It also seems odd, actually, that she could have been suffering in recent days and then have embarked on a journey to Coire Lagan this morning. Don't you think so?'

'I do.' Andrew nodded and looked even more thoughtful. 'Very odd. But you may be on to something. The doctors say something triggers the condition, but so far they have no idea what it is.'

'When did it start?'

'I'm not too sure.' He thought about it a moment and then added, 'About a year ago. She's been up and down ever since.'

'Let's hope the up stage lasts now,' Gwen said gently.

'Yes, indeed. Amen to that,' Andrew replied with a grimace.

# 33.

'You told me this morning, Gwen, that you were leaving partly because your work wasn't going well. What's the problem? What is it that you do, actually?'

'I'm a rug designer, Andrew. I work for an old, long-established family business in Leeds. I was in a road accident that put me out of action for a while, and I came here to continue with my convalescence and get back to doing some work. The internet makes that possible these days.'

'I see.' He nodded. 'And sketching, drawing, is part of that?'

'Well . . . ' She screwed her face up as she considered how best to answer. 'Not normally. Most of the work is done on computers these days, but I fancied getting back to basics for a change. I always enjoyed having a pencil in my hand and a clean sheet of paper in front of me. It's how I started doing designs.'

'Me, too,' Andrew said. 'Not rug design, though,' he added quickly. 'I mean, I always liked drawing. I still do, not that I do much of it these days.'

She frowned. 'Oh, yes! Malcolm, I think it was, said you make elaborate staircases. Surely that must start with a design?'

'I used to make 'em,' he admitted. 'Not now, though. Not for a while. What I meant was, I always liked just drawing. I was good at it at school, and so on.'

'And went on to art school?'

'Yes.' He looked surprised. 'Did Malcolm tell you that, as well?'

'Probably. Somebody did,' she said airily. 'Malcolm — or your mother, perhaps. Edinburgh, wasn't it?'

Brow furrowed, as if it were a difficult thing to contemplate, Andrew nodded. 'Edinburgh, yes. But Dundee first. What about you? Did you go to art school?'

'I could have done, but no, I didn't. I took a different route. I went to university in Leeds, and studied textile engineering. It's a good department, and long-established.

'I didn't really want to do fine art. I thought that would make me an art critic or art historian rather than a painter. I wanted to do something more practical.'

'And that ambition transmorphed into rug design?'

She laughed. 'Eventually, yes. I found my niche.'

'Lucky you. Are you good at it?'

She laughed. 'Of course! Fazackerly Brothers wouldn't retain me if I wasn't.'

He recited the name of her employer to himself and smiled. 'I like the sound of them,' he said with a smile. 'Nice and old-fashioned. No wonder their rug designer works with pencil and paper.'

She laughed again and said, 'How about some coffee? Might we have some, do you think?'

'Sorry!' Andrew jumped up and reached for the kettle. 'Not much of a host, am I? I can't even offer you a glass of wine.'

She shook her head. 'A simple cup of instant coffee is what I crave. Anyway, how about you and your work? Have you found your niche yet? Is it staircases?'

He pondered the question while he waited for the kettle to heat up. She smiled. His seriousness was really quite endearing. Everything had to be carefully considered.

'Like you, I decided eventually that I wanted to do something more practical than studying the Old Masters. I didn't really care much for contemporary art, either. Unmade beds, stuffed sharks, videos of grass growing — all that sort of thing.

'But I was always good at working with wood, and eventually I found my way into staircase-making. I found I liked it. The work was very satisfying. And, yes, I was good at it. So I guess that was my niche.'

'How on earth did it happen?'

'By accident, really. I took a casual job one summer, working for a builder who was putting up new houses. To start with, I helped a joiner who was building staircases. They saw I was good at it and put me on that full-time. I liked the work, and it got me thinking.

'At the end of the summer, I decided to try to start up in business for myself — as a staircase designer and builder. I got a commission from a man having a big house built outside Portree. The guy liked what I did for him. He was in business himself, and advised me to advertise and promote my services. He said there were opportunities out there, and he was right. For a time, I did very well, and enjoyed what I was doing.'

He stopped his narrative while he made the coffee. Gwen sensed he was at the end of it anyway. In a way, she knew the rest. The roof had fallen in on his personal life. Eventually, he had come back to Glenbrittle with Fiona, and here they both were.

'What's the problem with your work?' he asked, going back to where they had started. 'You said it wasn't going very well.'

She blew out her cheeks, wondering how to explain. It was difficult, but she wanted to make the effort. She felt she was talking to someone who was capable of understanding. Incredibly, she seemed to have found almost a kindred spirit, they were so like-minded.

'I've done quite a bit while I've been here,' she started off. 'And they seem to like what I've done so far, back in Leeds. But it's not what I hoped to achieve.'

'In what way?'

'Well, for want of a better word, it's not very inspired. What I've done is more of the same, when I hoped to find a rich new seam that I had never explored before.'

'What are we talking about here? Materials, pattern, colour, or what?'

'Colour and texture, principally. Pattern, too, of course. And materials. But mostly what I hoped to find here were natural things that I hadn't considered using before.'

'Sea, sky, heather — that sort of thing?'

'Well, yes. Natural things that I could look at and use in a different way. Oh, it's too vague and complicated to explain. I'm not doing very well, am I?'

He paused before he said anything else, thinking it through. 'I understand, I think, to a point. But I would understand even better if I could see what you've got so far. Are you really leaving tomorrow?'

'Yes,' she said. 'I am. Most of my stuff is packed up now, and I'm ready to go.'

He said nothing to that, but she thought she could hear him thinking it was a pity. In a way, so it was.

# 34

She had thought of phoning Rob to tell him she was coming home, but she was too tired by the time she got back to the cottage. A conversation with Rob would inevitably be emotional and long, and she just wasn't in the mood, however much she was looking forward to seeing him again. Tomorrow was going to be a long day if she did the journey in one go. Better to wait till she got home and had recovered.

Tired as she was, she couldn't get to sleep that night. She lay awake for hours, processing the events of the day. They were going round and round in her head. It was as if she was still living them.

Most of all, of course, she was so blissfully happy that nothing bad had happened to Fiona. It had been such a relief to know that she had guessed right about where the child had headed, and an even bigger relief that they had found her before she was anything worse than cold and wet. She could so easily have wandered off the edge of a cliff in the cloud.

Even now, the memory of how helpless she herself had felt when the cloud wrapped itself around them made her shiver. Luckily, Andrew had always known where they were, and which way to go. She had depended absolutely on him when they were on the mountain. Her part had been to guess where Fiona had gone. And she had done a good job there, even if she did say so herself!

Surprisingly — and this was another reason for feeling relieved — Fiona had been in good spirits despite her ordeal. In fact, Gwen thought with a smile, she had been pretty excited that she had managed to bring them both running after her. It was as if she had had a plan, and it had worked. Well, in the short term it had. Gwen sighed. She just hoped Fiona wouldn't be too downhearted when she discovered she was still leaving.

Then she smiled. How endearing, and lovely, that she wanted Gwen to be her new mummy. Whatever had put that idea in her head? Such a fantasy!

But, when you thought about it, it was easy to see where it had come from: her ongoing longing to be a part of a proper family, and a child's conception of what a happy family looked like. Fiona had been peopling her drawings with the people she knew and liked. Nothing wrong with that, so long as reality wasn't too crushing a disappointment.

She turned over and switched on the little lamp on the bedside table to see what time it was. Heavens! One-thirty — and she still hadn't been to sleep.

Then there was Andrew, she thought, her mind still refusing to close down. What a lot she had learned about that strange man today — or yesterday, rather. There was a lot more to him than she had thought. He was far more pleasant than she had first supposed, too. In fact, he had been remarkably good company all day, despite the huge pressure he had been under when Fiona was missing. He had stood up to things very well, she decided. Good for him!

★ ★ ★

In the morning, after a few hours' sleep at last, she completed her packing. Then she phoned Mrs McIver, and managed to reach her this time.

'I've been away at the hospital so much,' Mrs McIver explained. 'That's why you've not been able to get me.'

'Your husband?'

'Indeed. He's had a bad spell again.'

'I hope he's improving?'

'Well, he's a bit better than he was, which isn't saying an awful lot. But you've got to look on the bright side, haven't you?'

Indeed you had. Gwen agreed with

that. There wasn't much else she, or anyone else, could do.

Then she told Mrs McIver of her own change of plans. In advance, she had decided she couldn't leave the poor woman in the lurch. So far as Mrs McIver was concerned, the cottage had been let for the whole summer, and she would have been turning away other prospective clients. Gwen had no intention of leaving her out of pocket. She would continue paying for the cottage as agreed until someone else rented it.

Mrs McIver was dubious, and no doubt both disappointed and relieved. Gwen worked hard to reassure her.

'So I'll leave the key with Malcolm,' she concluded.

'Then, if you come back from time to time, you can just pick it up again, can't you, dear?'

Gwen hadn't the heart to say that wasn't going to happen. It was easier just to agree.

Afterwards, she had a last cup of coffee. Then, finally, she was ready to depart. That was when someone knocked on the door. She assumed it was Malcolm, come to save her the journey to the campsite office. His mother would have been on the phone to him already, no doubt.

But she was wrong. She had two visitors, not one.

'Hello!'

'We've come to say goodbye,' Andrew said, 'and to wish you a safe journey. Fiona wanted to see you again before you left. We both did.'

'That's kind of you. Thank you,' she said, feeling very flustered by their surprise appearance.

Fiona suddenly stepped forward and wrapped her arms around Gwen. She hugged her hard.

With a lump in her throat, Gwen knelt down and gave her a kiss. She could think of nothing to say, nothing appropriate. Fiona was obviously distressed by her impending departure.

'I hope you're feeling well this morning, Fiona?'

The little girl nodded, and then blurted out, 'But I don't want you to go!'

'Now, Fiona!' Andrew said sternly. 'We agreed we wouldn't do that. Gwen has enough to think about.'

'It's all right, Andrew,' Gwen said, shaking her head. 'I understand.'

Turning back to Fiona, she said, 'I shall miss you, sweetheart. But I have to go home now. I will write to you, though. I'll keep in touch.'

Fiona nodded bravely and stepped back.

'I'll just leave the key with you, Andrew. I was going to drop it off with Malcolm, but perhaps you can save me the journey?'

'Sure.'

He held out his hand. She took it, and leaned forward to peck him on the cheek. He hugged her quickly. Then she kissed Fiona again and headed for the car.

# 35

It was a long way back to Yorkshire. Her time in Glenbrittle had wiped the length of the journey to get there from her memory. Now she rediscovered just how long it was, and how long it took. Having driven for ten hours, and covered well over two hundred miles, she turned off the M6 and took refuge in a hotel on the edge of Carlisle. She couldn't possibly go any further, and from a safety perspective had probably already driven too far anyway.

Driving had taken her mind off things and engaged all her attention. Once she stopped driving, though, an awful lot flooded into her head. The recent past vied for her attention with the near future. She was still rehearsing what had happened with Fiona and Andrew while she tried to sort out what she was going to say to her parents and

Rob. The latter, Rob, had to be her priority now, but she was too tired to think straight about how she would tell him she had changed her mind.

She decided to have a meal in the restaurant attached to the hotel and then try to get a good night's sleep. The morning would be soon enough to think of the future. She would do it when she was fresh and wide awake. Tonight she could afford to luxuriate in memories of Glenbrittle and little Fiona, and perhaps Fiona's father too.

Such a strange, complicated man, Andrew, she thought just before sleep finally claimed her. Interesting, too. She wondered what he would have said about her work, had she got round to showing him some of what she had been doing. Perhaps he would have suggested a motif of staircases? Wooden staircases flying through the heavens! Something to think about, she decided with a smile.

In the morning she continued her journey down the M6 and turned off towards Kirby Lonsdale. At last she was approaching home territory. Nearly there now.

She waited for the familiar upsurge of pleasure and joy as she neared home, her parents' house. It didn't come. When she finally switched off the engine outside the home she had known all her life, she still didn't feel enthused. She was looking forward to seeing her mum and dad, but . . . But what? She didn't know. She only knew that something was missing. She wasn't very excited.

'Hello!' she called as she opened the front door. 'Are you here, Mum?'

A screech from the kitchen told her the answer. She smiled as feet thundered through from the back of the house.

'Gwen! What on earth . . . ? Oh, let me hug you!'

They settled at the kitchen table with a pot of tea. Mum wanted to know everything. How was she? How was her leg? How was Skye? What had she been doing? What was she going to do now?'

Gwen laughed. 'It's lovely to see you, Mum. It really is. How am I? You can see for yourself how I am. Tired at the moment after the drive, but fit and well. Lately, this old leg has been doing amazing things, too.'

'Is it better?'

'Do you know, Mum, I really think it is. It has been for some, actually. I've just needed to build up some fitness and strength, and some confidence. I've been doing that by walking. Glenbrittle is such a wonderful location from that point of view.'

'Ah!' Mum said nostalgically. 'I remember it so well. It's such a long time since we were last there, as well. I don't know why. We'll have to ask your dad when he gets home.'

'Come again. You can stay with me,' Gwen said without thought.

'Oh? So you're going back there, are you?'

Gwen hesitated. Having been put on the spot, what was she to say? All the doubts and uncertainties came to the front of her mind.

'Well, I wasn't. But I don't know now, to be honest.'

'There's Rob to think of, I suppose. Wouldn't he like Skye?'

'What would he do for a job, Mum?'

'Ah! There is that, I suppose. I wasn't thinking.'

Rob worked as an account manager in advertising for *The Yorkshire Post*. It was a good job, although Gwen couldn't claim to know much about it. She was even less interested. Not her thing at all. But she couldn't imagine Rob being eager to give it up and take his chances on Skye with a local weekly paper.

In any case, now she was here, she was suddenly unsure what to do about Rob. She had come all this way partly in order to see him again, and now she found herself wondering if it was what she really wanted to do. What am I like? she wondered despairingly.

'Mum, there's something I need to

tell you. I broke it off with Rob a while ago.'

'Oh? You didn't say!'

She shrugged. 'I don't know why I didn't, really. Perhaps I was just keeping my options open.'

'Can I ask why? You've been together a long time. Mind you, I did wonder what you going to Skye alone was all about.'

'The accident gave me a lot of time to think. I was on my own so much, especially at night. One of the things I decided was that I didn't want to continue with Rob. That's it, really.'

'Poor Rob. He's always thought so much of you. Was it the accident?'

Gwen shrugged. 'Perhaps that came into it. I don't really know. I forgave him, though. I'm not holding that against him.'

She sighed and added, 'I just knew I didn't love him, not enough to want to spend the rest of my life with him.'

'It's a good thing, then. You've done right. It's better to find out now than in ten years' time.'

'Thank you, Mum.'

'What about now? Will you see him now?'

She shook her head. 'It's a funny thing, Mum. I came all this way thinking I would, and even that we might make up again, but now I'm here I don't want to do that. Rob is part of my past, not my future.

'It wouldn't be fair on him to pay him a visit either. He's got to make a different life for himself, just as I have.'

Mum laid a hand on top of Gwen's where it rested on the table. 'There's no-one else, no other man in your life?'

She shook her head. 'No. That is, not really. Not in the sense you mean.

'But very recently I've got to know an interesting man called Andrew. He works on the campsite, and has a lovely little daughter called Fiona.'

'Oh? Works on a campsite?'

'At the moment he does. I think things have been difficult for him for quite a while, as he's a single parent.

But he's a craftsman, really. He designs and builds beautiful staircases. Or he did, until he had to look after his daughter full-time.'

'That's different!'

'Isn't it? But, as I said, there's nothing romantic going on between us. I just find him interesting, and I rather like him. But it's his daughter I know best. She's a lovely little thing, and she comes to see me every day nearly to do some drawing.'

'A man with a daughter, though,' Mum said thoughtfully, as if troubled by the idea.

'Oh, you don't need to worry, Mum! I don't think Andrew is interested in me in the slightest. And I'm not really all that interested in him.'

Mum smiled, and seemed about to suggest she thought otherwise. Then she sat up straight at the sound of the front door opening. 'Here's Dad now! He'll be so surprised to see you.'

Gwen smiled happily. 'And I'm so looking forward to seeing him.'

# 36

She spent a second night at home with her parents, and then she set off back to Skye. It was what she wanted to do more than anything. The urge to return was overwhelmingly strong. Seemingly, all she had needed to do to discover that was make a brief visit home to Yorkshire. She knew now that there was too much unfinished business in Glenbrittle for her to want to be anywhere else on earth.

Again, she broke the journey. This time, she pushed on further the first day and stayed overnight in a guesthouse in Fort William. From there, it was an easy drive up to Invergarry and then down Glen Shiel to Kyle of Lochalsh.

And there it was again: the magical Isle of Skye! The mountain peaks were tantalisingly clad in thick cloud when she caught her first glimpse, but everywhere else was bathed in the pure light of a summer morning.

She felt a shiver of excitement as she crossed the Skye bridge. What would she find back in Glenbrittle? How were they all? And the cottage! She had only been away a couple of days, but already she longed to see it again. How glad she was now that she had kept the tenancy. It would have been terrible if she hadn't been able to return to it.

And Fiona. How she looked forward to surprising her. Not only that. Fiona, she had convinced herself, would be well if she was there. Although she had not said so when Andrew was talking about it, she didn't believe it was coincidence that Fiona's condition had disappeared when she took up residence in the cottage in Glenbrittle. Nor did she believe it was coincidence when a relapse occurred after Fiona heard that she was to leave.

If it comes to that, she thought, why did Fiona's condition only develop after the departure of Andrew's wife a year ago?

Well, the doctors might be mystified, but she wasn't. Fiona was psychologically disturbed by the absence of a mother in her life. So far as Gwen was concerned, that was the explanation of Fiona's mysterious illness. No mystery about it. The only mystery was why no-one else, not even her own father, seemed to have thought of it.

So what was she planning to do?

Well, she couldn't literally be Fiona's mother, but there was a lot she could do. It might not be easy, but the way she felt was that her presence alone would help. They could resume their relationship, their friendship, and build on that. See if it helped. She was sure it would.

What else? Well, they could do some more sketching together. Perhaps they could take picnic lunches, and go with their pads and pencils to do some sketching outdoors. They would both enjoy that, she was sure. Always assuming, of course, that Andrew didn't object. She didn't think he would, but it would be better to take nothing for granted. She would talk to him about what she was thinking, and let him know what was happening from now on. It would be safer, and sensible.

What about Andrew himself? She shook her head and gave a wry smile. She didn't know. She just didn't know. Were they to be friends, after all? It was hard to say, let alone know. Until the other day it had seemed unlikely, but she would just have to see how it went now.

Most of the time she had been staying in the cottage, Andrew had been so difficult, and even downright unpleasant at times, but then things had changed. Their search for Fiona had brought them together, and after that he had been quite different. She had seen him in a totally different light.

Of course, it had all been to do with his fears over Fiona's disappearance. That had been the turning point. It might turn out to have been a temporary change that would now be reversed, but she didn't believe so. Something more significant had happened between them, and Andrew had seemed every bit as sad as Fiona was when they came to say goodbye. The very act of doing that had been a huge development in itself, and most unlike the Andrew she had thought she knew.

So, a temporary meeting of minds, perhaps? Or something more profound? She didn't really know. What she did know was that she wanted to find out for herself. That was a large part of why she was coming back to Glenbrittle.

\* \* \*

It was eagle-eyed Fiona, of course, who spotted her arrival. She was swinging on the campsite gate, and nearly fell off in her astonishment when she saw the familiar car turn off the lane and onto the short track leading up to the cottage. Gwen saw her, waved, and stopped the car. She opened the passenger door as Fiona came racing across towards her.

'Gwen!' she shrieked as she reached the open door. 'Oh, Gwen! I knew you would come back. I told Daddy, and I told Uncle Malcolm as well. I told them! I said you would.'

'Fiona! Hello, sweetheart,' Gwen said, laughing. 'So you told them, did you? How did you know? And what did they say?'

'I just knew. That's all,' Fiona announced as she climbed into the car and threw herself at Gwen, who hugged her hard. 'Daddy said he hoped I was right, and Uncle Malcolm said he didn't know. But I knew!'

'Well, you were right. And here I am. Come on! Let me get us back to the cottage.'

Fiona disengaged herself, and allowed Gwen to put the car in gear. 'Did you miss me?' she demanded. 'Like I missed you?'

'Oh, I did. Of course I did,' Gwen assured her.

'Every night?'

'I've only been gone two nights, Fiona.'

'Well, I missed you every night.'

'And I missed you, too. So it's a good thing for both of us that I've come back, isn't it?'

'Yes,' Fiona affirmed.

It was only when they reached the cottage that Gwen remembered she no longer had a key.

'I'll go and get it!' Fiona said. 'I'll tell Daddy you're here, as well.'

And off she went, like a little rocket. Gwen shook her head as she watched her go. No problems with her legs at all, she noticed with a smile.

It's true, she thought happily. I am good for her. And she's good for me. I really am pleased to see her again. I must have missed her more than I realised. How silly I am!

Then she dug in her pocket for a tissue. Suddenly a tear or two had unaccountably clouded her vision.

# 37

Fiona returned with Andrew, as well as the key.

'So you came back?' he said, smiling.

'Yes, I did. Couldn't stay away. Hello, Andrew!'

'Gwen.'

He held out his hand. She took it, and then leaned forward to peck him on the cheek. He gave her a hug.

'I said you would come back!' Fiona cried, dancing around them.

'She did, too,' Andrew admitted with a grin.

'Don't ask me why,' Gwen said, glancing up at the sky as raindrops began to patter all around them. 'It can't be because of the weather.'

'It's not much, this. Soon be over. Why don't you go inside and put the kettle on? We can start unloading the car for you.'

'Would you? Oh, thank you. That's a good idea.'

Soon the car was unloaded, the cottage opened up, and a pot of tea made. The three of them sat around the kitchen table. It was like old times, Gwen thought fondly, feeling she had been away for ages. Outside, the rain had settled into a steady downpour.

'Soon be over, Andrew?' Gwen teased, glancing through the window as she put the teapot down.

He shrugged and grinned. 'Soon enough. It won't last forever.'

'So, how is everybody?'

'Malcolm is busy. We all are at the camp-site, now we're into summer proper.'

'Summer?' she said with a shudder, glancing at the window again.

'It's our kind of summer. At least we have long days and short nights.'

Gwen chuckled. 'You're right. And it's still very beautiful. It was lovely coming over the Skye bridge, seeing the island again. It felt like a homecoming.'

He nodded. 'Good.'

'I like it here as well,' Fiona piped up, perhaps afraid she was being sidelined by their conversation. 'Especially when we do some drawing. Will we do some today, Gwen?'

'Perhaps not today, dear,' Gwen said, laughing. 'I'm too tired. But tomorrow afternoon we might. How would that be?'

Fiona considered the proposal carefully before giving it her approval.

'We'd better get going,' Andrew said, getting to his feet. 'I've got things to do, and so have you.'

'Well . . . '

She wasn't going to disagree. There were things to do, but most of all she wanted to lie down for half an hour and recover from two days in the car.

'Maybe tomorrow,' Andrew added thoughtfully, 'I could see some of your work? You didn't have time the other day.'

'Oh? You're still interested?'

He nodded.

'Then I can show you what I've been

up to while I've been here. Come with Fiona.'

He nodded. 'Till tomorrow, then. And welcome back!'

'Thank you, Andrew — and you, too, Fiona. It's good to be back.'

Afterwards, she wondered what to make of it all. It had been as easy with Andrew as it had been the day she left. So perhaps the rapprochement had not been a temporary suspension of hostilities. That was good news. Much as she wanted to continue seeing Fiona, she couldn't without her father's approval. As for Andrew himself, well, they would just have to see.

Fiona, though! Just the same, she thought with a grin. The same as ever. It had been lovely to see her again, and to see how much she had been missed. She hoped she could do a little more for her now, and not just regard Fiona's visits as a break from her own routine. She even wondered if she might be able to help Andrew a little with her home tuition.

But she ought to try to discourage Fiona from thinking of her as a sort of surrogate mother. It was perfectly understandable that a little girl like her longed to have a mother to cling to, and confide in, and serve all the other purposes that mothers the world over served, but she had to understand that Gwen wasn't going to be it. In time, as she got older, no doubt this phase would be put behind her.

Oh, well! she thought. That's enough for one day. Now I just want to sort a few things out in the cottage, make myself something to eat, and then get some sleep. That will do me for today. In the morning I'll find something to show Andrew when he comes with Fiona. He seems interested in what I do, and — who knows? — it might be useful to bounce ideas off somebody like him.

Somebody like Andrew? What exactly did that mean? she wondered. Andrew had built wooden staircases. That was a long way from making rugs. True. But he had some training behind him as a student of the fine arts, and she sensed he had an interest as well as a visual understanding. He was observant, too. So there might be something from him.

She yawned. I must crack on, she thought. Otherwise, I shall be falling asleep on top of all these boxes and bags. There'll be time enough tomorrow to think about Mr McIver and his daughter.

# 38

While Andrew leafed through a sheaf of her sketches, Gwen made cups of coffee, found a can of cola for Fiona, and then settled the little girl at one end of the table with her drawing implements and a big sheet of blank paper.

'See what you can come up with, Fiona,' Gwen urged. 'Perhaps something different this time?'

Fiona nodded. Then, tongue dangerously between teeth, she drew a straight line across the page. Gwen arched her eyebrows and stepped back.

'I see what you're after,' Andrew called.

She carried the cup of coffee over to him. 'You do, do you?' she said, smiling. 'Most of the time, that's more than I can.'

'It's pretty clear,' Andrew insisted, frowning with concentration as he peered at a sheet where she had pulled together different images.

Gwen sipped her coffee. 'Oh?'

'Colour, texture, pattern. Like you said. Natural materials. Earth tones. Lines. I can see how you're thinking.'

He was, Gwen realised, quite stimulated by what he could see. He leant forward, scrutinising her sketches closely.

'Then you transfer the images, and try to develop patterns based on them. Colour's important, too. But can you produce wool to match? It is wool you use?'

'It is, yes. Until now, mostly sheep's wool from New Zealand.'

'Why not Yorkshire wool? Or Skye wool?'

She shrugged. 'Custom. Tradition. A consensus that New Zealand merino wool is superior to home-grown wool.'

'And is it?'

'Sometimes I do wonder,' she said with a sigh. 'But I think it probably is. Purity is a big thing about it. That makes it better when it comes to the dyeing.

265

Wool produced in this country has a black thread running through it, whereas New Zealand wool is a very pure white.

'And it wears well, and is nice and soft. So Fazackerly's has always been happy to use it, like most other luxury wool and carpet makers. Anyway, it's difficult to change people's thinking, when what they've been doing for a long time works fine.'

'Business people?'

She nodded, chuckled, and added, 'And sometimes it's difficult to change your own thinking!'

Andrew smiled and went back to turning pages. 'Going back to the problem you said you had, can you be more specific about it?'

She shrugged. 'Not really. If I knew what was wrong, I could fix it.'

He nodded. 'I understand.'

After another moment's consideration, he added, 'I don't know anything about rug making, of course, but I like your sketches. They're good. They're real! They stand out from the page to me. I like the range and variety. I can see how you might make patterns from them. At least, I think I can.'

'You're right. I can. I have done, in fact. That's not the problem.'

'What is, then?'

'How can I put it? They're . . . Well, they're just more ordinary than I had hoped. More of the same. They lack the inspiration I came here to discover. They're perfectly usable — some of them, at least. The studio manager has even said so. But they don't excite me. There's nothing new,' she finished limply.

Andrew thought for a moment. 'Leave it with me,' he said, for all the world like an instructor in an art class. 'I'll see if I can help.'

'That would be nice!' Gwen said with a smile.

She moved over to see how Fiona was getting on with her latest drawing of an imaginary happy family.

'Two dogs, Fiona?'

The little girl nodded and took on an

intent expression. 'Benjamin needed company,' she said in all seriousness. 'He was a little bored on his own all the time.'

'I see,' Gwen said, wondering if there was a metaphor in there somewhere.

A knocking at the door brought her head around. 'I wonder who that can be?

'Malcolm, probably,' Andrew said, getting to his feet. 'I'll go.'

But it wasn't Malcolm. He was wrong about that. When he returned, he said, 'You're wanted.'

'Oh? Who is it?'

He just shook his head. With a puzzled frown, she hurried to the front door.

'Ellen!'

'Gwen. Have you got a minute?'

'Of course. Come in.'

'You've got company. Can you step outside for a moment.'

Gwen hesitated. The last time Ellen had had private words for her had not been a pleasant experience.

'Please.'

'What is it?' Gwen asked, stepping out into the garden.

'I didn't want to talk in front of Andrew.'

Ellen turned away and stared into the distance. Then she spun round and took a deep breath.

'Gwen, I feel such a fool. I don't know what got into me. I'm so, so sorry about what I said to you about Malcolm. I know now what was going on. Malcolm told me when he gave me his birthday present. You'd been helping him.'

Gwen nodded, and smiled. 'That's true.'

Ellen sighed and added, 'Then, when I heard you'd left, I felt absolutely terrible. I knew it was all my fault. Gwen, I'm so, so sorry. That just wasn't like me. Not at all. I must have been having a terribly bad day.

'I'm not trying to make excuses, Gwen, but please believe me when I say I've been devastated by my own

269

stupidity. I didn't know what to do about it either. As soon as Malcolm said you had come back, I rushed over to see you.'

Gwen smiled with relief and gave her a hug. 'Don't worry about it, Ellen. As it happens, I was having a bad day myself. Andrew had told me off about Fiona being here. So when you started as well, it just felt like everybody had fallen out with me.'

'So I'm forgiven?'

'Of course.' Gwen smiled. 'I soon realised why you'd gone off like that, but I couldn't defend myself without spoiling Malcolm's surprise for you. Anyway, I had other things on my mind. I couldn't deal with everything at once.'

'And now you've come back?'

'I was only away a couple of days, Ellen! Yes, I've come back. Andrew and Fiona are here at the moment. Are you coming in to see them?'

Ellen shook her head. 'Another time, if you don't mind. I just wanted to apologise.'

'No need, Ellen. Really. You've been a good friend ever since I arrived.'

'Apart from that day.'

Gwen laughed, feeling genuinely relieved. 'It was a one-off,' she said. 'Let's just forget it.'

# 39

Everything was different now: the same, yet different. She knew now that she had not been mistaken. Her misgivings and doubts had been overcome. There was a place, and a role, for her here.

The same but different? Oh, Glenbrittle was outwardly the same. The Cuillins were still there, and the sea. The campsite, too, although with more tents and people now that summer was advancing. Fiona came most days, if not quite every day. It depended on visits to, and by, her grandmother.

So little had changed objectively. But Gwen was in love now, and she knew it. She felt, too, that Andrew was as attracted to her as she was to him. Nothing had been explicitly said or done to prove it. But she knew. The signs were all there. She just had to be patient, and give their developing relationship time.

So, although nothing much had changed, everything had changed. The world was bigger and brighter now, and so full of promise.

\* \* \*

Walking along the beach together one evening, while Fiona ran on ahead, Gwen raised a subject to which she had been giving much thought.

'Why don't you show me your workshop, Andrew?'

'Why? What makes you ask that?'

'I'd like to see what you do there. You've seen what I do. Now it's my turn.'

Chuckling, he said, 'I don't do anything there now. I haven't for some time.'

'No. I understand that. But you used to, and you might again one day, mightn't you?'

He sighed. 'I don't know about that. It doesn't seem very likely.'

'I'd like to see it anyway. I might get some ideas.'

'For your rugs?' he said, laughing. 'Ideas from wood?'

'Why not? Who knows?'

'OK,' he said, giving in. He shook his head, pretending to be completely uncomprehending. 'How about tomorrow? I'm free then.'

'Tomorrow would be fine.'

\* \* \*

The workshop was in another property owned by the McIver family, an old, stone-built boat shed just behind the quayside in Portree. Andrew opened up the big door at the front, ushered her inside, and switched on some lights. She looked around with surprise and delight.

'How wonderful! Andrew, you could live here.'

'Yes,' he said dubiously. 'I have thought of it. But a lot of work would need doing first.'

274

She managed to avoid asking the obvious question: What's wrong with that?

Instead, she took a few moments to orient herself. Where they stood was a big, open space, which must have been ideal for boat building, sheltered from the weather. The floor was made of stone slabs, and the roof of slates. A roughly worked staircase at one end led to an upper storey for part of the building.

'What's up there?' she asked, pointing.

'Rooms. A number of them. Full of junk from my grandfather's boat-building days.'

'Was that the family tradition?'

Andrew nodded. 'That's how come we have this property down at the harbour.'

'It must be where your woodworking skills come from,' she said with a smile. 'It's in your genes.'

'Maybe it is, but none of my staircases are fit for going to sea.'

Laughing, Gwen asked if there were windows upstairs.

'A couple. Mostly it's skylights.'

She nodded and let her eyes continue their roaming. It was a fascinating place, reminding her of ancient parts of the Fazackerly's mill in Leeds. Stone and wood, tools and materials. Things being built and made. The only item missing was noise. This was very definitely a workshop fallen into disuse.

'It's too quiet,' she said. 'I would like to hear hammers and saws, machinery running, men whistling and shouting.'

Andrew laughed and pointed at a timber structure on one side of the workshop.

'Nobody's working here at the moment, but that's a part-built staircase. It's a while since I did any work on it, though, and I don't know when, or even if, it will ever get finished. I keep thinking I ought to give the guy that ordered it a phone call, and tell him to find someone else to do the job for him.'

'Oh, I wouldn't do that!' Gwen said sharply. 'Keep your options open, Andrew. A day will come when you can think of completing it.'

'You think?' he said, sounding highly sceptical.

Her eyes turned to the unfinished project that Andrew had mentioned. 'So this is your work in progress?'

He nodded. 'It used to be.'

The timber structure was one section of what looked as if it was going to be an absolutely enormous staircase. Gwen walked across to examine it. She could see immediately how much detailed work had gone into it. Joints and seams were barely visible. When she gently tested the banister, nothing moved at all.

'Impressive,' she said, running her hand along the polished surface of the wood. 'It's oak, isn't it?'

'Yeah. Nothing but the best, although this modern oak is not like the timber that built Nelson's battleships. It's all imported. Mostly yellow oak.'

'Which isn't as good, I take it?'

He shook his head. 'Good enough, though. The staircase will probably still be there when the house is so old it falls down. Or it would have been,' he added.

'You should finish it, Andrew. You really should.'

She stepped back and let her eye range over the length of the structure. It was broad and sleek, with clean lines that ached to have a hand smoothed along the rail, or a small child sliding down the banister. She smiled with appreciation and shook her head.

'It's absolutely beautiful. But what a size it will be!'

'Yeah. This is just one section, the most difficult to make.'

'How long did it take you?'

He shrugged. 'A couple of months. I don't remember exactly now. But the whole thing was supposed to take six months.'

'It must be for a very big house?'

'A country hotel. Their staircase is Victorian, and falling to bits. Cheap wood and poor workmanship in the first place. This was supposed to be a legacy statement.'

She turned and looked around the workshop. There were carefully arranged stacks of timber on one side, each length separated from the next by wooden spacers.

'Is that everything you need?' she asked, nodding at the stacks.

'Pretty much. Apart from time, of course. But you can't import that.'

'No,' she agreed, thinking hard.

What a pity that it seemed work had stopped. What on earth was Andrew doing, messing about on a campsite when he was so skilled a craftsman he could build such a beautiful thing as this?

*   *   *

Afterwards they had lunch in a small café with Ellen, who escaped from the bank for an hour. Gwen was pleased her friend was available. She hadn't seen so much of her in recent weeks. Thankfully, Ellen and Andrew were cordial to each other, which was a lot better than Gwen had feared it might be.

Ellen gushed on about how she was decorating her flat, which was a major DIY experience for her.

'I didn't even know which way to open a tin of paint,' she explained proudly. 'In fact, I didn't even know which way was up.'

'If you can read the writing on the tin,' Andrew said solemnly, 'it's the right way up.'

For a moment, Gwen held her breath.

'Thank you, Andrew!' Ellen said, laughing and looking surprised. 'I'll remember that.'

Gwen let out her breath with relief. She had forgotten until then how little Ellen thought of Andrew, and vice versa. Lunch might well have been a major disaster.

'I thought I hadn't been seeing so much of you, Gwen,' Ellen said, leaning across the table, making a show of excluding Andrew and speaking in a confidential tone. 'Are you two an item now?'

'Ssh!' Gwen whispered, embarrassed, risking a nervous glance at Andrew.

'Yes,' he said with a smile. 'I believe we are, aren't we, Gwen?'

'Yes.' She returned the smile and shrugged at Ellen. 'It was supposed to be a secret.'

Ellen positively beamed. 'Good! I'm so glad, Andrew, that you've found someone sensible at last — someone who can keep you in order.'

'So am I,' Andrew said with a grin. 'So am I.'

Gwen smiled happily at them both.

On the way home, Andrew stopped the Land Rover and said, 'Now we've spoken to Ellen, would it be all right to kiss you?'

'As if you haven't already?'

'As if,' he said solemnly.

She laughed hysterically and smothered him with little kisses. Then he took her in his arms and kissed her properly, and she knew then for sure that everything would be all right between them.

# 40

A day or two later Andrew asked Gwen if she would like to visit Coire Lagan.

'I'd love to, Andrew. You know I would.'

'Tomorrow, then. The forecast is good. We can make an early start.'

'How early?'

He laughed and shook his head. 'You city people! Let's plan to leave about nine. That suit you?'

'That sounds fine.'

'Good. You nearly got there when we were looking for Fiona. So you know you can do it.'

'Yes,' she said with surprise. 'Do you know, I never even thought about whether or not I could do it that day? We just went, didn't we?' He nodded. 'So I don't have to worry now.'

'Another thing,' he added. 'I think I may be able to help you with your work problem.'

'Oh? Tell me more!'

'Tomorrow,' he said. 'Let's leave it till tomorrow. I've got to get back to see to Fiona just now.'

'Tomorrow, then,' she said with a smile. 'By the way, is Fiona going with us?'

He pulled a face and shook his head.

'She'll really want to go, Andrew.'

'I know, but there's the problem with her legs to think about.'

'Let her go. She'll be fine.'

He studied her for a moment. 'This is your theory that she's OK when you're around?'

Gwen just smiled. 'Let her go, Andrew.'

⋆ ⋆ ⋆

The day dawned bright and clear. Well into June now, the weather was more settled. It was cool first thing, but Gwen could see the sun was probably going to have its way with the Cuillins all day long. Glorious, flaming June! she thought. How lucky I am to be here.

Then she thought of Fiona, and wondered if she would be going with them. She hoped she would, but it was down to Andrew. So far as Gwen was concerned, though, she was confident that Fiona really would be able to manage the climb. After all, she had almost reached Coire Lagan on her own that famous day. Besides, she actually believed in the theory she had confided to a doubtful Andrew. It wasn't a coincidence that Fiona's health and fitness were fine when she was around. It really wasn't.

Oh, dear! she thought with a wry smile. I do hope I'm right, and not just indulging myself in megalomania.

Andrew came for her soon after eight-thirty — together with Fiona.

'I'm coming, too!' the little girl trilled.

'Hello, dear! That's good. I thought you might like to see Coire Lagan at long last.'

'Yes.' Fiona nodded and looked

serious for a moment. 'I nearly got there myself, didn't I?'

'You did. I remember that very well. It will be better if we all go together, though, won't it?'

Fiona gave a shy smile and nodded.

Gwen glanced at Andrew, who winked at her. She smiled and nodded. All was well. They would try it together, and hopefully do it together.

They got away just before nine. Andrew set a steady pace and Fiona stayed close to him, clearly intent on demonstrating her ability to keep up. Gwen struggled for a while, but gradually she worked the stiffness out of her body and managed not to lag too far behind.

Andrew glanced back at one point, realised what was happening, and slowed down. 'Sorry!' he called to her with a chuckle. 'A bit too fast for you?'

'Not at all,' Gwen assured him with a grin. 'Do your worst. Fiona and I will keep up, won't we Fiona?'

'I'll try,' Fiona promised.

'That's my girl!'

Andrew kept to a more comfortable pace for them both after that.

'How are your parents, Andrew?' Gwen asked.

'Much the same as for some time now. Dad's in pretty poor shape, unfortunately, but Mum's fit as a fiddle.'

'What is it your father suffers from?'

'It's his heart. He's pretty frail now. In and out of the hospital all the time. But Mum keeps things going.'

'Helped by you and Malcolm?'

He nodded. 'Mal and I look after the holiday cottages. We're lucky, as a family, to have the business. I don't know how we would manage financially otherwise. Especially me. A life on benefits wouldn't be much fun.'

'What about the cottage you and Fiona live in? That's not owned by the family, is it?'

He shook his head. 'No, unfortunately. I've got it on lease from the estate. It's been very handy, but the lease runs out shortly. We'll have to find somewhere else.'

To Gwen, it seemed a strange, transient way to live, with no settled work or home. He did have Fiona and his family, of course. Perhaps that was enough?

Anyway, how the McIvers made their living wasn't so uncommon these days. Right through the highlands and islands, tourism was so important now that there must be many people living on the summer proceeds from campsites and holiday cottages. Living better, too, than when their livelihood came from growing potatoes and raising a few sheep, with a bit of fishing to go with it. She didn't suppose crofting had ever been as wonderful as the romantics liked to make out.

They climbed the hillside behind the campsite and kept on heading uphill, following a well-trodden path up towards the mountain ridge high above. Their path crossed other tracks meandering along the contours of the hillside, but it was difficult to know if they had been made by walkers or by sheep. Gwen was happy to leave route-finding in the hands of a local expert.

Soon after crossing one of the transverse paths, Andrew said, 'Now we're on the route we were following when we were looking for Fiona.'

'Goodness! Were we as high as this?' Gwen asked, panting with the effort of their sustained climb.

'Quite a bit higher, actually. Let's stop for a minute. Catch our breath.'

They sat down on a big rock, looked around, and gazed down into the glen far below.

'You did really well getting all the way up here on your own, Fiona,' Gwen said, shaking her head.

'Yes, I did,' Fiona agreed, 'but it was very hard work.'

'And dangerous,' Andrew pointed out severely. 'You shouldn't have done it on your own. But Gwen's right. You did do well. You're doing well today, too. How are your legs?'

'All right, thank you.'

'No pain?' Gwen asked.

Fiona shook her head.

'They don't feel weak?'

'No.' Then she qualified her answer. 'They're a bit tired, though.'

'So are mine,' Gwen assured her with a chuckle.

Andrew caught Gwen's eye. She nodded and smiled. They both knew how well Fiona was doing. Long may it last, Gwen thought.

They had been climbing for an hour when Andrew said, 'We're halfway there. A bit further, actually.'

Gwen nodded but didn't reply. Conversation was not quite beyond her, but her breathlessness made it difficult. She was very warm now, too, and beginning to flag from the effort she was making. Her thigh muscles were aching. So were her shoulders and her back — and everything else! The backpack that had seemed so easy to lift and carry initially was now almost unbearably heavy, even though it had little in it beyond her jacket, a couple of sandwiches, and a water bottle.

Despite her growing fatigue and pain, she was confident she could carry on for a good while yet. At least as long as little Fiona, she hoped! Her time on Skye, and the walking she had done, had made her so much fitter and given her the confidence to accept the physical challenge.

And Fiona was a wonderful example to follow. She seemed inexhaustible. To be young again! Gwen thought ruefully. Why on earth did she and Andrew ever doubt Fiona's capabilities?

The path degenerated into a rocky scramble, and the mountains began to close in all around them. Gwen guessed they were approaching the entrance to the corrie. That seemed to put fresh energy into her legs and back, and she forged on with grim determination. She could do this!

Sgurr Alasdair was looking ever more formidable in the shadows at the head of the corrie, and on their left flank Sgurr Dearg was a steep wall of bare rock bathed in harsh sunlight. There was no way she was ready for either of them, she knew. But maybe one day . . .

They pressed on. The tireless Andrew kept them moving steadily, and maintained a close eye on his charges. Gwen sensed he was very aware of how they were doing at all times, without making ostentatious efforts to help Fiona or herself. She was glad of that. She would have hated to feel like a hapless passenger. But she knew there would be a ready helping hand if either she or Fiona needed it.

Suddenly, Andrew stopped and said, 'We're here.'

# 41

Her head came up and she paused to look around. Immediately ahead was a short, and very steep, rocky slope. Beyond that, she couldn't see at the moment. Andrew was already tackling the slope, with Fiona close behind. She followed, climbed over the crest and then came to a stop, astonished by the view ahead.

It was no longer a vista of jagged, shattered rock. Great, bulging tongues of smooth rock seemed poised to pour down on them. The slabs stretched from one side of the entrance to the corrie to the other. Gwen marvelled at their shape and extent, and at the sense of sheer power underlying them. There was no doubt at all what they were. They were a huge fossilized lava flow.

'Oh, Andrew! How wonderful.'

Fiona whooped with delight and

Andrew gave her a hug. Then he turned and grinned at Gwen. 'Worth coming to see?' he called.

'Oh, yes!'

'I thought you might like it up here. This is a very special place.'

She got moving again, and climbed up to join him. 'It's tremendous. You can just see and feel how the molten rock was flowing. It's almost as if it's still moving now!'

Andrew nodded. ''Boiler plates', they're called. Great, steaming outpourings of basalt and I don't know what else. We're in the cauldron here. Come on! Let's explore.'

With Fiona in the lead now, they walked up and over the great boiler plates. The rock was so coarse and granular that friction grabbed at the soles of their boots, wouldn't let go, and made it possible to walk up steep slopes that normally would have had them on their hands and knees.

Gwen laughed with delight at the strange experience. Fiona, in her excitement, began to perform intricate little dances until Andrew put a stop to that.

'Careful!' he warned. 'Slip now, and you'll be back down at the campsite before you can catch your breath.'

'Daddy's right, Fiona,' Gwen said, chuckling. 'We'd both better try to be sensible while we're here.'

Fortunately, Fiona wasn't a child you had tell twice. She just grinned and calmed down.

Gwen made the mistake of drawing the back of her hand experimentally across the face of a boulder. 'Ouch!' She winced and pulled her hand away.

'I should have warned you,' Andrew said with a grimace.

'It's so sharp!'

'Yes, it is. The famous Skye gabbro. Great for rock climbers — until they fall off, of course. Then it's like sliding down a cheese grater.'

Gwen dropped to her knees to examine a jagged vein of quartz that ran all the way across the rock platform on which they were standing. In places, the pure white quartz exhibited huge, perfectly formed crystals that looked pristine fresh.

'How long has it been here?' she asked wonderingly.

Andrew shook his head. 'I can't remember, exactly. But quite a few million years. Fifty million? Something like that.'

She shook her head in awe. 'It could have arrived just this morning. See, Fiona!' she added, pointing to a little basket of crystals. 'How beautiful they are.'

'We could draw them,' Fiona said, crouching down to look closer.

'Indeed we could. Let me take a photo to remind us later what they're like.'

Gwen worked her camera and then stood up straight, turned, and waved her arm around at the massive walls of rock encircling them. 'It could have happened just a few days ago,' she said, marvelling.

The waves of lava had cascaded from

somewhere higher up, one overtaking another until there was a whole series of them, overlapping as they cascaded down the mountain side.

'Come on!' Andrew said. 'I've got something else to show you. You haven't seen the lochan yet.'

They made their way uphill, moving carefully over and across the boiler plates until they reached their highest point. Then, at last, the lochan, the small lake in the centre of Coire Lagan, came into view. Perfectly still, it sat there, shimmering in the sunlight.

'Oh, my! How beautiful,' Gwen exclaimed softly.

Fiona whooped and raced down towards the water's edge.

Andrew smiled, satisfied.

*   *   *

They sat in silence for a while, eating their sandwiches and pouring coffee from their flasks. Gwen studied the lochan, and processed what they had just seen.

She felt excited, visually stimulated. She had never seen anything like the rock formations here. The little lake, yes. It was beautiful, certainly, but she had seen other beautiful mountain lakes. Those frozen lava flows, though! She had never seen anything like them.

Fiona went off to play at the edge of the lake. They watched her hopping from one dry rock to another, until she tired of doing that and started skimming flat pebbles across the surface of the water.

'She's never still, is she?' Gwen said.

'Never.'

'Where does she get her energy?'

He shook his head. 'How come her legs are not troubling her today? That's what I want to know.'

'Oh, well. You know the answer to that one. I told you.'

He grinned. 'You did. And I'm beginning to think you might be right.'

'I'm sure of it. There's nothing wrong with her physically at all. Oh, I'm so glad you brought me here, Andrew,' she added. 'I'm so happy!' She leant sideways and kissed him on the cheek. 'Thank you!'

He laughed and put an arm around her to give her a hug.

'I thought you would like it,' he admitted. 'I even hoped Coire Lagan might give you some fresh ideas — some of that inspiration you've been looking for.'

'With reason. It would be a poor artist, or craftsperson, that didn't feel excited by this place. In fact, it would be a poor human being.'

'My thinking exactly.'

It was extraordinary, she thought fondly, not for the first time, how they had so much in common. This difficult, awkward man seemed to see the world through eyes very like her own. Who would have thought it?

They stayed there by the water's edge for another hour. Andrew talked about his love of the Cuillins in general, and of this place in particular. He pointed out the great stone chute, the tourist route to the summit of Sgurr Alasdair that didn't involve rock-climbing. Then his finger travelled along the ridge and he picked out the nearby peaks, as he told her about the challenge of traversing the whole of the Cuillin ridge in one go. He himself had done it twice, once in early summer — the usual time to tackle it — and once in winter, when the whole ridge was sheathed in snow and ice.

Gwen listened spellbound. She loved the way he spoke so modestly of his achievements in the mountains. She felt she could have listened all day, and the day after, too. But, eventually, it was time to leave and to start their descent.

'Maybe one day you would like to try Alasdair itself?' Andrew suggested.

'Could I manage it, do you think?'

'Comfortably,' he assured her. 'You're fit enough now. Your problems are behind you.'

'Can I go, too?' Fiona wanted to know.

'Yes,' Gwen assured her. 'When we go, we will all go together.'

⋆   ⋆   ⋆

They made it back to the campsite in half the time it had taken them to climb up to Coire Lagan. Fiona looked exhausted by then, and Gwen was very tired — but happily so.

'What a wonderful day it's been, Andrew.'

'Perhaps it could be the first of many?' he suggested, with that wonderful smile she was coming to know so well.

She smiled back. 'I'm sure of it,' she said happily, taking hold of him by the hand that wasn't clasping Fiona's.

# 42

Gwen was thoroughly engrossed for the next few days in transcribing images from her head and her camera onto paper and her laptop, and then pushing them around into new patterns that could be brought to life in textile. The process was both creative and intensive, and it was a good long while since she had been so excited about her work. The rock formations up at Coire Lagan had given her material to work with she had never even considered before, and she wanted to strike while it was all so fresh in her brain and eye.

Bulging, tumbling, frozen, molten rock shapes, and coarse, crystalline surfaces were what had thrilled her. So to start with she worked now on flat, grey surfaces with jagged lines of pure crystalline quartz zig-zagging through them at random. The drawings and photos were transferred to her laptop, and there she began to play with them in earnest.

By the time Andrew visited her a couple of days later, she had assembled a significant body of work, some of which she had already emailed off to the studio in Leeds, where Dr Blenkinsop was always ready to look at her design offerings. 'What do you think?' she had asked, giving nothing away about her own feelings.

'How's it going?' Andrew wanted to know, after giving her a hug and a kiss. 'We haven't seen you around for a few days.'

But he knows, she thought happily. He knows exactly why that is. He ought to! He's responsible.

'So-so,' she said with a grin.

'No better than that?'

She laughed and swatted him with a rolled-up magazine. 'You know how it is, Andrew! I'm in the zone. You led me to a treasure trove and opened the door. Since then there haven't been enough hours in the day for me to get everything down before it fades.'

'We could go back again?'

'We could. We will, in fact. Of course we will. But I wanted to work with my first impressions — that red-hot feeling you get when you see something for the first time?'

'And have you done that?'

'I've made a good start. Just this afternoon I emailed some stuff off to the head of design back in Leeds. I need to hear what he thinks.'

Andrew nodded and looked solemn for a moment. 'You're in the zone.'

'Yep.'

'Could I see anything? Or is it too soon?'

'No, it isn't. Sit down. Where's herself, by the way?'

'She's been out with her grand-mother all day. I think they're getting something to eat right now. But she'll come by in a little while.'

'Good.' Gwen smiled and added, 'I haven't seen her for ages.'

'Two days.'

'Like I said — ages.'

Andrew took a seat. 'So let me see what you've been doing.'

'Yes. But later we need to talk, Andrew. Soon, I mean. We need to talk — seriously. Right?'

He nodded, looking solemn, and said, 'I agree. I think we do. It's time, isn't it?'

'Indeed it is.'

She let him leaf through the sheaves of drawings. Then she set up her laptop and took him through what she had there. Surprisingly, perhaps, she felt no inhibitions about showing him work in progress. She sensed that only good could come of it.

He said at last, 'You got such a lot out of Coire Lagan, didn't you? Far more than I expected. I'm impressed.'

She shrugged and then grinned at him. 'Thanks to you!'

'No. You would have found your way there sooner or later.'

Perhaps, she thought, but the reality

was that we went there together: the two of us and Fiona. We saw and we shared. We listened. All that was an important part of the experience.

'Andrew, our visit to Coire Lagan was a turning point for me,' she said.

'For me, too,' Andrew said quietly, gazing intently at her.

That was the moment Gwen realised things really had changed, and not only for her. Hesitating only for a moment, she moved in close and stooped to wrap her arms around him. He pulled her to him, and kissed her long and hard.

'Hello! I'm here.'

'She's here,' Andrew said, rolling his eyes in mock desperation.

Gwen laughed and pulled herself away from him.

'Come in, Fiona!' she called.

The door burst open, and there she was, brimming with happiness and excitement, if looking a little dishevelled. Gwen gave her a hug and then stood back to look at her.

'You're a little untidy, Fiona,' she said

uncertainly, straightening the little girl's coat collar and smoothing her hair.

'That's 'cause I've been running. I came as fast as I could!'

'No need for that, sweetheart. Take your time. Catch your breath.'

'Have I missed anything?' Fiona demanded.

'Not a thing,' Andrew said.

Gwen gave him a push. 'Possibly nothing that you don't know about, Fiona.'

'What does that mean?' the little girl demanded.

Confused, caught unawares, Gwen took refuge in searching for a drink for her. She would have liked to say more but Fiona had arrived too soon. She wasn't ready. Perhaps her father could deal with the situation.

'Where's Gran?' Andrew asked, getting to his feet. 'I wanted a word with her.'

'Talking to Uncle Malcolm at the shop.'

'Right. You'll have to excuse me,

Gwen,' he said, glancing at her.

'Of course. Fiona will keep me company. But do come back — if you can?'

'In half an hour,' he said with a smile. 'Be good!' he added for Fiona's benefit.

'Now, Fiona,' Gwen said when Andrew had gone, 'tell me all about your day.'

She did. At great length. She told Gwen absolutely everything. And it took all the time there was until Andrew returned.

# 43

So engrossed was she in following Fiona's detailed account of her day that she almost missed the ringing of the phone.

'The telephone!' Fiona trilled.

Gwen jumped up, laughing. 'It's a good thing you're here, Fiona. I would have missed it. I wonder who it can be.'

She picked up the phone.

'Hello, Gwen. George Blenkinsop here.'

'George! Hello. How nice to hear you. How are you?'

'The same. As grumpy as ever. How about you? Feeling recovered yet?'

'I am, George. Thank you. I'm pretty good now. I've even started going up mountains.'

'I wondered about that. Is that where these latest patterns have come from?'

'It is. Yes.'

She wondered what was going to come next. It was unusual for George, the head of design at Fazackerly's, to phone like this. It hadn't happened before, not since she'd been in Glenbrittle.

'I thought so.'

'What did you think, George?'

'About the patterns?'

'Well, yes. We've done my health, and yours. What about the patterns?'

There was a short pause, during which she held her breath. Then George said, 'I think they're great, Gwen. They're right up there with your very best work, if not better. I decided to phone to congratulate you, since you're ensconced on that Godforsaken island and I'm unlikely ever to see you again.'

'Oh, George!' She laughed. 'You say the sweetest things.'

'Never heard that before, but I'll take it.'

George went on to say they could work with the new designs, and were eager to make a start. What were her plans? When was she coming back to Leeds?

'I'm not really sure,' she said hesitantly. 'That is to say . . . '

'You've got a feller up there, have you? Is that what you're trying to tell me?'

She blushed as she laughed. 'Do you know, George, I just might have. It's early days yet, but it looks promising.'

'Good. It's about time you settled down.'

'Very kind of you to say so, George. Thank you lots.'

'Oh, you know me, love! Proper Tyke, through and through. Speak my mind. Say what I really think. Always have done. Can't change now.'

'Thank goodness for that! I wouldn't want you to change.'

'I'm glad we're agreed on that. So sort your life out, Gwen. No need to hurry back here. We can make a start without you. Besides, there's not much that can't be done these days online, if we can also get together from time to time for consultation. Let's just agree to stay in touch for now, shall we?'

'Absolutely, George. And thank you!'

Right, she thought afterwards, metaphorically rolling up her sleeves. That's me sorted. Now for Andrew.

★ ★ ★

The opportunity arose a little later, after Andrew had returned and they all three went out for a walk along the beach. Fiona had run on ahead, eager to be the first person to leave footprints on the blank canvas left by the retreating tide.

Gwen decided to approach things head-on, like a true Yorkshire lass, the female equivalent of George Blenkinsop.

'I've been thinking, Andrew.'

'Do you expect me to be impressed?'

'Now, now! No sarcasm, please.'

She took his hand as they walked along the beach. 'I think you should go back to designing and building staircases. Anyone can do what you do here at the campsite. You're a highly skilled and talented man. You should get back to what you're good at.'

'Is that it? What you've come up with, after so much thinking?'

It was said with a rueful chuckle.

'That's only one of the things I've been thinking,' she said firmly, refusing to take the bait. 'I know the problems, the obstacles in the way, but they can be overcome.'

'How?'

She smiled at him. 'It's time for that discussion we've been promising to have, isn't it? Then we can deal with the 'how' question you've just asked.'

He laughed. 'Go on,' he suggested.

'Well, unless I've got it all wrong, we're going to be together from now on — all three of us — aren't we?'

Head on one side, she looked at him and waited.

'It's what I would like,' he agreed. 'You know how I feel about you.'

'I do. And you know I love you very much.'

He nodded. 'On a good day, I think I do.'

'Be sure of it,' she said firmly.

'Agreed.'

'Right. So now we've got that settled, let's deal with the rest of it. Where are we to live, for example?'

Andrew chuckled and sat down on one of the big rocks at the far end of the beach. 'What do you suggest?'

His lacklustre attitude wasn't what she had expected. Something was wrong. She could see that.

'You said the lease on your cottage runs out soon. Why not move into mine? Your family owns it, after all. I'm sure we could reach agreement with your mother.'

'What about your job?' he asked, still in a desultory manner.

'That's OK, as well. It's agreed. I can stay here, with occasional visits to Leeds.'

He stared out to sea. She waited. Patience seemed to be required. She had known that all along. He was a complex man.

'They're off out early,' he remarked.

Her eyes followed his, out to a small fishing boat that was making its way out to sea.

'Are they?'

He nodded. 'They must be going a long way out. Something's caught their attention. A big shoal of herring, perhaps.'

'Yes,' she said without much interest.

'You're very good for me, Gwen,' he said suddenly. 'And I love you dearly. But I come with an awful lot of baggage. We've never really talked about that, have we?'

'Are you talking about Fiona?' Gwen said with a chuckle. 'She's a precious cargo, Andrew — not baggage!'

'Indeed she is,' he acknowledged with a reluctant smile.

Both pairs of eyes swung then to search for Fiona, a distant speck of animated colour at the edge of the wet sand.

'That little girl has brightened my life, Andrew, and I love her dearly. You don't need to worry about Fiona being with us.'

'I know that. She feels the same about you.'

'So are you thinking about something else? Her departed mother, perhaps? Or your departed wife?'

He nodded and glanced at her anxiously. 'You know about them?'

'I do.' She shrugged. 'Not everything, perhaps, but enough. All I need to know. Ellen and Malcolm have both talked about them, and I've picked up things from other people as well.

'Tell me more, if you wish. But it won't make any difference. My mind is settled, and so is my heart.'

He talked about his past then, and at some length, but without adding anything significant to what Gwen already knew. She let him go on, feeling it was important to let him have his say.

When finally he ran dry, she laid her head against his shoulder and said, 'Nothing you have said makes any difference, Andrew. I love both you and Fiona too much. But I appreciate your telling me.

'Just remember,' she said gently. 'Whatever the difficulties, love will find a way.'

He smiled again at last. 'Thank you. I was worried. I thought you might change your mind when you knew what you what were getting into.'

'Kiss me,' she commanded.

'Now,' she said briskly, a minute or two later, 'what's to stop you making staircases again?'

'Looking after Fiona, for a start. I can't be both here with her, and in the workshop, or on site, with a staircase.'

'I'll be here every day,' Gwen said. 'She can be with me some of the time. I'll keep an eye on her. Perhaps Malcolm and your mother will help, too.'

Andrew nodded. 'But then there's her education. I can't be educating Fiona and building staircases at the same time, can I?'

'I can help with that, as well,' Gwen said briskly.

Even as she said it, though, she realised this was a good opportunity to raise something she had been thinking about for a while.

'Fiona's education is something I think you ought to reconsider, Andrew. Whatever was the case when you and Fiona first came here, it's different now. Fiona is not a physically or psychologically fragile child any more, thanks to you, and perhaps in a small way to me, too. She's a well-adjusted, properly functioning, perfectly capable little girl. All she needs now is ... Well, you probably know yourself, don't you?'

He nodded. 'You think she should attend school, don't you?'

'I do,' Gwen said firmly. 'She needs to be growing up and making friends with other children she sees every day of her life. Here, she's in an adult world all the time.'

'There are plenty of kids around the campsite.'

'Only in the summer, and even then how many stay for more than a week, two at the most? For most of the year she'll scarcely see another child.'

'You're right,' he said with a sigh.

'I've been thinking that myself for some time. So what shall we do?'

Gwen liked that, the 'we' in his question. It made her feel she truly belonged in the world of Andrew and Fiona.

'Short-term, we can take her either to where she can pick up a school bus or all the way to school. Portree, would it be? Or a village a bit nearer? I don't know where the schools are.

'Anyway, Perhaps Malcolm, and one or two others, could help a bit with the transport. We could organise a rota.

'Long-term, here's something else I've been thinking about. How about converting part of your workshop building back into a living space? You said your grandparents used to live there. Perhaps we could do it again? The cottage here could be for weekends, or when it suited us. What do you think?'

Andrew mulled it over and began to laugh.

'What?' she demanded anxiously.

He shook his head. 'I needed someone like you in my life,' he said. 'You've got it all worked out, haven't you?'

'Not quite, but . . . '

'You have,' he said firmly. 'Let's do it!'

'Let's ask the person who all this will affect the most,' Gwen suggested, as Fiona came racing across the sand towards them.

Fiona dug in her heels and screeched to a stop. Then she looked from one to the other of them, suspiciously at first, and then with a big smile.

She knows, Gwen thought with amusement. She knows everything. Perhaps she always did know.

'Fiona, you know that big, happy family you like drawing? The one with lots of children, and dogs and cats and things?'

'Yes?' Fiona said with a knowing smile.

'Well, do you think it might be possible to be happy in just a small family? To start with, at least. Just you, and a mummy and daddy?'

Fiona squealed with delight and threw herself into Gwen's arms. Then

## BITTER IS THE DUST

### Scott A. Gese

When Sarah McKinney finally escapes the clutches of her abusive husband, she and her adopted son Jason begin a perilous new life on the run. Eventually they settle down as Sarah finds work as a doctor's assistant, and Jason is reunited with his real father and takes a job as a ranch hand. But Jason's quick temper soon gets him into trouble with his employer, and their future hangs in the balance as their unhappy past threatens to catch up with them.

# FORTRESS IRON EYES

## Rory Black

Tracking outlaws Dobie Miller and Waldo Schmitt into a deadly desert, the notorious bounty hunter Iron Eyes is closing the distance between them with every beat of his determined heart. Yet the magnificent palomino stallion beneath his ornate saddle is starting to suffer. Every instinct tells Iron Eyes to stop his relentless hunt for the wanted outlaws. When he decides to risk following an Indian trail to a water source, his steely eyes spot something out in the sickening heat-haze: a towering fortress. Iron Eyes presses on . . .

Gwen felt Andrew put his arms around them both. Tears seemed imminent, but she had never felt happier. Whatever the difficulties, she reminded herself, love will find a way. Of that, she was quite certain.

We do hope that you have enjoyed reading this large print book.

Did you know that all of our titles are available for purchase?

We publish a wide range of high quality large print books including:
**Romances, Mysteries, Classics**
**General Fiction**
**Non Fiction and Westerns**

Special interest titles available in large print are:
**The Little Oxford Dictionary**
**Music Book, Song Book**
**Hymn Book, Service Book**

Also available from us courtesy of Oxford University Press:
**Young Readers' Dictionary**
**(large print edition)**
**Young Readers' Thesaurus**
**(large print edition)**

For further information or a free brochure, please contact us at:
**Ulverscroft Large Print Books Ltd.,**
**The Green, Bradgate Road, Anstey,**
**Leicester, LE7 7FU, England.**
**Tel:** (00 44) **0116 236 4325**
**Fax:** (00 44) **0116 234 0205**